"Nessa?" Mitch frowned at her with desire-heavy eyes.

"Don't call me that! And please...don't touch me again."

"Come again?"

Vanessa shook her head, too emotionally swamped to put her feelings into words.

Mitch took a step toward her, but she moved, keeping the distance between them. "Ah, honey."

"It's over between us, Mitch. And I'm not interested in any reminiscing."

"What *is* your problem? I want you—you want me. Nothing's changed!"

ALISON KELLY, a self-confessed sports junkie, plays netball, volleyball and touch football, and lives in Australia's Hunter Valley. She has three children and the type of husband women tell their daughters doesn't exist in real life! He's not only a better cook than Alison, but he isn't afraid of vacuum cleaners, washing machines or supermarkets. Which is just as well, otherwise this book would have been written by a starving woman in a pigsty!

Books by Alison Kelly

Alison Kelly has a warm, witty writing style you'll love! Bubbly heroines, gorgeous laid-back heroes...romances brimming over with sex appeal!

ALISON KELLY

Progress of Passion

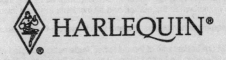

HARLEQUIN®

TORONTO • NEW YORK • LONDON
AMSTERDAM • PARIS • SYDNEY • HAMBURG
STOCKHOLM • ATHENS • TOKYO • MILAN • MADRID
PRAGUE • WARSAW • BUDAPEST • AUCKLAND

For Kim
a loyal, loving friend
who always listens with her heart

ISBN 0-373-18708-4

PROGRESS OF PASSION

First North American Publication 1999.

Copyright © 1995 by Alison Kelly.

Look us up on-line at: http://www.romance.net

Printed in U.S.A.

CHAPTER ONE

'A *WHAT*?'

Although Vanessa identified with the stunned disbelief in her ex-husband's voice, her body's response to his easy country drawl, even after ten years, was all too familiar. That he could still physically disturb her, even across telephone lines, worried her far more than she cared to admit.

'I'm going to be a *what*?'

'*Grandfather*! You're going to be a grandfather, dammit!' she snapped, then quickly covered the mouthpiece so Mitch wouldn't hear her sniffles and know she was crying. Why, as a liberated divorcee of the nineties, was she having such a hard time dealing with the fact that her daughter was going to be a mother? She sniffed again and tried to concentrate on what Mitch was saying.

'*Angie's pregnant*?'

'Well, since she's the only child you have, who else is going to make you a grandpa?' Vanessa asked, irritated that even when he was asking stupid questions Mitch still managed to sound like the sexiest man alive.

'Vanessa, are you *sure*? How did it happen?'

'How? I'll give you a clue, Mitch; it wasn't an immaculate conception!'

'Listen here, Vanessa, you're her mother—'

'It's good to know at thirty-eight you still have the facility for total recall.'

'Put Angie on,' he demanded.

'She's asleep at the moment.'

'Then wake her! I want to talk to her.'

'Tomorrow. We'll be at Brayburn tomorrow afternoon.'

'Tomorrow! Where are you now?' Mitch's tone clearly implied that he'd assumed she was calling from Perth.

'Tamworth. We arrived in Sydney this morning.'

'You're here? You're coming to Brayburn?' It seemed he found her presence more disturbing than the reason behind it.

'This is something the three of us needed to discuss face to face, but even so I'd hardly expect you to leave your precious cattle and fly to Perth!'

'Still singing the same old song, uh, Vanessa?'

At his weary response, she silently cursed herself for being churlish.

'Look, Mitch, I'm tired. I'm not up to discussing this right now; I'll see you tomorrow. Goodnight.' She severed the connection before he could prolong the conversation.

Grateful for the custom that saw all Australian motels regardless of size and grandeur providing tea-and-coffee-making facilities for patrons, Vanessa turned on the room's electric jug then sought out the industrial-strength headache pills she always carried when travelling. She'd never been comfortable flying and avoided it whenever possible; however her current situation hadn't allowed for her to drive the width of Australia and today she'd endured the stress of not only the flight from Perth to Sydney, but also a second one to Tamworth.

The tightness in her neck hinted at her muscles 'going into spasm', but only someone who didn't know the details of her relationship with her ex-husband would attribute her discomfort to the stress of flying.

'Rot in hell, Mitch Randall!' she muttered, furious that after all these years he still had the power to affect her physically. Of course there was a gulf of difference between the sensual bliss he'd created in the past and the muscular tension for which he was currently responsible!

She swallowed two tablets, then popped a third into her

mouth just for good measure—if she didn't manage at least *some* sleep tonight, she'd be in no shape to face the two-hour drive to Brayburn, much less Mitch.

After stirring a token amount of milk into her tea, she carried the cup back to the double bed and rested it on the night stand, while she pulled back the covers and crawled beneath them. The sound of soft, even breathing drew her eyes to where her daughter slept in the single bed on the other side of the room.

Angela's black hair contrasted with the stark whiteness of the motel's serviceable white sheet, just as her dark lashes contrasted with the flawless beauty of the girl's young skin.

Vanessa felt her heart tighten as, deep in sleep, Angela snuggled further beneath the covers until only the top of her jet-black head was visible. It was a habit she'd developed as a child and for years Vanessa had crept into the child's room several times a night to lower the blankets, terrified her little girl would smother. Again she felt the sting of tears; all too soon her little girl had become a woman. All too soon she would be a mother.

It seemed incredible that only three days ago Vanessa's most worrying problem had been whether it was viable to increase the number of designer labels she carried in her Perth boutique. Now she was having to deal with the fact that her eighteen-year-old daughter was pregnant and that history was repeating itself in a particularly warped way.

'Oh, Angela,' she whispered, 'if there was anything I hoped would never happen to you, it was this. You're just a baby yourself. *My* baby.'

Quickly she pressed a hand over her mouth and nose to smother a sob, afraid she'd wake her daughter. The last thing she wanted was for Angie to feel she'd let her down, because Vanessa had experienced first-hand the pain and guilt of knowing she'd fallen well short of her own parents' expectations.

Besides, she wasn't disappointed *in* Angie—she was disappointed *for* her. It wasn't fair that this should happen. It just wasn't damn well *fair*!

Determined to pull herself together, Vanessa reached for the cup of now tepid tea and finished it in two huge gulps before turning off the lamp.

She wasn't going to fall apart, she vowed, mopping her nose with a tissue, not now, and not tomorrow when she had to face Mitch for the first time in a decade. She was going to stand by her daughter and help her every step of the way, whether she decided to keep the child or have it adopted out. In truth Vanessa was very uncomfortable with the idea of her grandchild being surrendered for adoption, but she recognised that the final decision had to be entirely Angie's. Vanessa, would support her to the end and discourage any over-indulgence in self-pity; self-recrimination, she reminded herself, blowing her nose, and tears weren't going to do a damn bit of good! She was an intelligent, successful thirty-five-year-old woman and, and…and—oh, lord! She was going to be a grandmother!

The valley was quilted with long, swaying grass, occasionally shaded beneath old twisted gum trees, and the lush greenness stretching to the horizon of mountains was a happy contrast to the drought-brown colour it had been when Vanessa had last driven this road ten years before. She too had changed.

She'd come a long way from the frightened, tearful young woman who had packed her eight-year-old daughter and two pieces of luggage into a car and sped away from Brayburn and her girlish dreams without so much as a note. She'd established herself as a competent, well respected business-woman once she'd learned to stand alone and out of the shadows of domineering males such as her father and Mitch Randall.

'Dad's going to freak.' Angela's soft voice cut into her thoughts.

'It won't be as bad as you imagine,' Vanessa said, tactfully refraining from pointing out that given the circumstances Angie was stating the obvious. 'He's had the forewarning of my call last night, and you know your father loves you too much to be angry with you for long.'

'It's not me I'm worried about,' the teenager replied. 'It's Craig.'

Vanessa tried to produce a reassuring smile, but was fairly certain she hadn't managed it. Just the mention of the boy responsible for her daughter's condition had her clamping her teeth together. She couldn't help it. Even though she'd never met the guy, the fact that he was employed as a stockman on Brayburn was enough to freeze her blood and send her mind fossicking through nineteen-year-old memories.

Fifteen minutes later, as a white gate rushed at her car, she was jolted back to the present.

Gripping the wheel fiercely, she pressed her foot on the brake to bring the car to a dust-churning halt. She eyed the neatly lettered sign above the gate.

BRAYBURN
Founded 1893 by C. & W. Brayburn.
Owners M. Randall & V. Brayburn.

Her stomach flip-flopped and knocked her heart against her ribs. It must have hurt, because there were tears in her eyes.

'Angie, open the gate,' she said, not taking her gaze from the sign.

'Oh, good! For a second there I thought you were going to just plough straight through it.'

Vanessa didn't reply to her daughter's sarcasm because she wasn't sure any words could possibly work their way around the lump that had wedged itself in her throat. She hadn't been prepared for the crippling nostalgia and sentiment she was experiencing.

'Mum, are you OK?'

'Uh? Oh, yeah, sure. I'm fine, honey,' Vanessa said, making a show of stretching her arms above her head. 'Just a bit stiff. Why don't you drive the rest of the way to the house and I'll get the gates?' That, she thought, will give me a chance to burn off this sudden surge of nervous energy.

'I'm not going straight up to the house,' Angie replied firmly. 'I want to see Craig first.'

'But that could take ages. This place is over a hundred square miles; he could be working anywhere!'

'Just drop me at the banding yards, OK? I'll find him.'

'But you have to see your father first,' Vanessa said, not sure that was absolutely necessary, but knowing *she* didn't particularly want to face Mitch alone.

'No, I have to see my baby's father first. Please, Mum, don't pressure me now?'

Vanessa wanted to argue the point, but one look at her daughter's face stopped her. There was nothing to be gained by upsetting her now. They were both too emotional and weary to discuss things rationally. On top of that, Angie seemed to be reaching the stage in her pregnancy when crying was a reflex action to everything from a bad joke to a chipped fingernail.

'OK,' Vanessa surrendered. 'We'll go to the branding yards first.'

They passed through five more gates before reaching the dirt road which lead to the area where the young calves were branded. When Vanessa would have turned off Angie told her to stop.

'Why? I thought we were going to find Craig.'

'No, Mum, I want to go by myself. I'll see you and Daddy up at the house later.'

'But Angie...'

'I want to tell him myself.' The girl opened the door and climbed from the car.

Vanessa was torn by the need to mother her daughter and the knowledge that as an adult this was something Angie had to do herself.

'Are you sure?'

'I'll be fine, Mum,' Angie said, then gave her a sly smile. 'Besides, did anyone hold your hand when you told Dad about me?'

Vanessa was too stunned to respond to the teenager's laughing farewell; instead she wrapped her arms across the top of the steering-wheel and rested her forehead on them. Memories of a young Mitch Randall flashed through her mind, dozens of them, but the one which loomed larger than life was of Mitch down on one knee asking her to marry him... immediately after she'd told him she was pregnant.

'Oh, God, please don't let that happen. Don't let a small mistake lead to an even bigger one. I love her too much to watch her have her heart broken.'

Again she felt warm tears slide down her cheeks, and it was some time before she could brace herself emotionally and re-commence driving in the direction of her most painful past.

She saw Mitch the moment she entered the main yard surrounding the house and knew, by the way his tall, muscular frame tensed momentarily, that he knew it was her.

Although he was only a metre or two away, it was impossible to see his face in the shadow of the wide-brimmed, dusty Akubra he wore. He was talking to a pudgy middle-aged stockman, who only served to make Mitch's six-foot-two frame seem perfectly proportioned and enhance the deliciously snug fit of his fawn moleskins. He had the longest legs God ever put on a man, she thought, remembering how it had felt to have her own wrapped tightly around them...

He turned his full attention to her and she felt herself give a guilty start. He strode towards the car and stopped two feet away.

'Where's Angela?'

She wanted to ask what had happened to the traditional 'G'day' as a form of welcome, but found her mouth couldn't function. Actually, she wasn't sure her lungs were working too well either, since breathing seemed impossible, but darn it her heart was working overtime! She would not let this happen. She would not let her attraction to this man trample all over her common sense!

'Well, where is she?' he demanded again, propping his arm on the roof of the car.

'She wanted to…take a short walk. She'll be here soon.'

The line of his mouth showed he wasn't impressed and Vanessa was glad she'd not told him where exactly Angie had gone. It wouldn't do anyone any good if Mitch went off after her and caused a scene. He seemed about to say something, but glanced over to the stockman he'd been speaking with and stepped back from the car.

'Go on into the house, Vanessa. I'll be with you directly.' He turned and walked back to the stockman.

A sense of disappointment hit her and accompanied her up the steps of the wide veranda, even as she tried to ignore it. Well what had she expected…a red carpet?

When she'd walked out on him ten years ago her actions had prompted locals to cast Mitch in the role of the *victim*. Even the letters from the few close friends she'd had in the region had been more sympathetic to him than her. It was ironic that when she had been the one who would have welcomed the support it had fallen to Mitch, who resented being perceived as the underdog in anything. Vanessa knew that if she still carried a lot of residual resentment over the demise of her marriage, it was naïve to expect that Mitch wouldn't.

She only hoped that they could keep it buried for the few days she and Angie would be here.

After not having seen each other or spoken more than twenty words together in ten years, the atmosphere when Mitch finally entered the house was stilted to say the least.

One look at his tense stance told her he was as uncomfortable with her presence as she was being there, but the resigned look on his face said that, given the circumstances, he was prepared to tolerate it. But being alone with him was unsettling her already precariously balanced nerves and she gazed out of the window in the hope that Angela would put in an appearance soon.

'I'm having a hard time believing this,' he muttered.

Judging by the dark circles under his eyes, he'd not slept a wink since her phone call, but his brooding good looks seemed even more potent because of it.

'Believe me, Mitch, I know how you feel.'

'How could you let this happen?' he asked. 'You of all people?'

She swung to face him. 'Me!' Her voice emerged as as gasp even as outrage flooded her body. 'Me, of all...'

'You're her mother dammit!' He ran a frustrated hand through his thick black curls. 'If she was...was...sleeping around, why the flamin' hell didn't you have her on the Pill?'

'Angie wasn't *sleeping around*, as you so eloquently put it!' She was pleased to see him wince. 'I had no idea she was seriously involved with anyone. How could I...?'

'You're her mother—'

'So you keep saying! OK, I'm convinced! But it's not *Angie's* parentage that's the issue right now,' she said, tartly reminding Mitch he'd not so much as bothered to ask who the father was.

'Who is it?' he demanded to know through clenched teeth. 'I'll kill the bastard. I'll...'

Vanessa couldn't stop the almost hysterical giggle which erupted from her, but her ex-husband's killing glare did so most effectively.

'Sorry,' she muttered. 'It's just that I've heard those same words, delivered in exactly the same way, once before.'

A heavy silence dangled between them and Vanessa found she had to work hard to hold his gaze without flinching. Her heart picked up its pace and for a moment she was seventeen years old again and back in this very room with Mitch, telling her father that she was pregnant. She blinked away the beginnings of a tearful mist and the moment was gone.

'What happened between us is exactly the reason I'd have thought you would have moved heaven and earth to prevent the same thing happening to Angie. You live with her,' he accused. 'You should have been aware of what was going on, for God's sake! Hell, I only get to see her for about eight weeks a year.'

'Well, here's a newsflash, Mitch Randall! Angela got pregnant while she was living under *your* roof, not mine!'

'She hasn't been here since July!'

'Angie is four and a half months along.' Vanessa found no satisfaction in laying the blame at Mitch's feet; the pain dulling his blue, blue eyes and draining the colour from his handsome face wrenched her heart. 'She...she only told me a few days ago.'

He said nothing for several moments, then turned and pulled a bottle of Scotch and two tumblers from a cupboard. She watched as he poured a liberal amount of the spirit into each of the glasses.

'Here—if you feel half as shell-shocked as I do you'll need this.' He handed a drink to her, then stepped back and propped himself against the spotlessly clean stainless-steel sink.

'Why did she wait so long before saying anything? Did she think it would ''go away''?' He lifted defeated blue eyes to Vanessa's face.

They were the bluest eyes she'd ever seen, and no matter how she'd tried over the years she'd never been able to forget them. She shook her head and took a sip of her drink, hoping the bitter liquid would make her next words easier to say. God knew, hearing them from her daughter's lips three days ago had nearly torn her apart.

'Angie was afraid in view of what happened to us that we'd...that...we'd force her to have an abortion.'

'*She thought what?*'

'She waited until she knew terminating the pregnancy wasn't an option.'

Mitch spat out a succinct obscenity. Shock and hurt struggled for domination in his face, but he made no attempt to hide the tears welling in his eyes. His obvious distress made Vanessa wish she could hold him, but she forced herself to remain where she was as he asked the same heartbreaking question she herself had voiced only days earlier.

'How...how could she think such a thing?'

'Apparently that's what happened to a girl she knew and Angela wasn't prepared to chance it.' She took a steadying sip of her drink. 'I told her that regardless of the differences between you and me, Mitch, there was no way either of us would have demanded abortion as a solution. Deep down I think she always knew that. I think it just took her a while to work up the courage to tell me.'

Mitch stared distractedly out the window and offered no response. Uncomfortable with the need to console him, she searched for something to say to keep the silence at bay.

'I told her that whatever decision she makes is OK with me. I trust you feel the same? Mitch?'

'There's a lot to be considered. What about the father?' He swung his gaze back to her. '*Who the hell is the father*? It must be one of those young blokes she met when we flew to Broken Hill for Stacey Whiting's wedding—'

'No, Mitch, it—'

'They were related to the groom and...'

'It isn't—'

'Angie told me one of them was moving to Perth—'

'Mitch, will you just shut up for a minute!'

The shrillness of her tone surprised even herself and she took a deep breath before continuing in a more controlled voice.

'It's not anyone she met at the wedding of some wealthy grazier's daughter.'

She saw a spark of worry enter Mitch's eyes. He'd placed Angela on a pedestal from the moment she was born and nothing had ever been too good for her. He'd spoilt her, pampered her and showered her with unconditional love, just as Vanessa's own father had once done to her. Yet ultimately Vanessa had proven a disappointment to Jack Brayburn, and she only hoped Mitch wouldn't withdraw from Angie as her father had from her.

'Who?' he asked, his face expressionless.

'Craig O'Brien. He's one of your—'

'I know who he bloody is! I pay the bloke's wages! Of all the stupid, idiotic things that girl has done this takes the cake! A jackaroo! And a smartass to boot...'

She listened in silence as Mitch listed all the reasons why Craig O'Brien, stockman, wasn't good enough for his eighteen-year-old daughter. Again she was struck by the realisation that she'd heard it all before.

'...O'Brien is too bloody smart for his own good and too quick with his fists as well.' Mitch poured himself a second drink, without pausing in his recital of Craig O'Brien's seemingly endless list of faults. 'That damn kid could get himself into a fight playing the organ at church! This is Cam's bloody fault.'

Vanessa was forced from her silence by Mitch's totally ludicrous accusation.

'Cam's? How one earth can you hold your brother responsible?'

'He suggested I hire the kid. Cam's friendly with his family and when he heard Craig wanted to try his hand at raising beef cattle, he talked me into taking him on.' He gave a harsh humourless laugh. 'And I, being the dumb bunny that I was, agreed!' He swore softly running a hand over his face. 'I should have seen what was happening!'

'So you were aware that something was going on between Angie and this Craig O'Brien?'

'No. Yes.' A metallic ping pierced the air as he slammed his fist against the sink.

'Hell's bells, Vanessa! They went to the flicks a couple of times and they used to dance together at the local parties. But if you're asking whether I turned a blind eye while they went off together on "dirty weekends" then *no*. As far as I could tell there was no great passion flaring between them.'

'Obviously there was!' she countered. 'Although you were probably so obsessed with the sex-drive of your prize bulls that if they'd taken to cavorting naked in the living-room you wouldn't have noticed!'

'Look, if it makes you feel better to blame me and rake up old grievances, fine! Do it! But it seems to me that in the long run it's not going to do a damned bit of good.'

For several seconds neither spoke, as they engaged in rugged visual battle. Vanessa was determined not to cower under the intense scrutiny she was receiving. In the end it was Mitch who muttered a resigned curse and looked away.

'Do you mind if I make a cup of coffee?' she asked, anxious to break the silence. 'It's been a tiring day.'

'Help yourself,' he told her waving his hand to the small electric urn on the bench. 'If you want it percolated, you'll find what you need in the pantry. I'm going to find O'Brien.'

'Mitch, no!'

'No? I rather think it's about time he and I had a few words, don't you, Vanessa?'

'Please, Mitch I don't want Angie upset.'

'And I'll upset her?' Mitch stared hard at her.

'Please? Speak with Angela first. She wanted to tell Craig herself. That's where she is now—looking for him.'

'So to date she hadn't told him either?'

'No.' She turned away and busied herself with the coffee.

'One of us should have gone with her,' he said.

'I suggested that, but she asked if I'd had a cheer squad when I told you I was expecting her.' Vanessa swallowed the lump that rose in her throat. 'I have a feeling we're going to have to face the fact that the precedent we set is going to be thrown back at us.'

Behind her Mitch made no verbal response and she wasn't ready to turn around and to gauge what his physical reaction to her words had been. The last thing she wanted was for them to be fighting tooth and nail when Angie arrived back. No, she thought, that's the second last thing I want. The last thing I want is to be feeling the very same attraction I've always felt around Mitch, but damn it, I am!

'H-h-hi, Dad.'

Angela's tentative greeting impacted into the silence with the effect of a large explosion and had Vanessa whirling round to face the kitchen door. A tall, rangy young man stood holding his daughter's hand, and his unexpected presence immediately sent Vanessa's gaze to Mitch. He looked livid. In fact he looked...

'Mitch, no!'

'Daddy, don't!'

Both Vanessa's and Angela's appeals counted for nought as in one fluid motion Mitch seized the younger man by the front of his shirt and slammed him out through the screen door and on to the veranda amid a string of bar-room expletives.

In the few seconds it took mother and daughter to sprint from the kitchen, in the wake of the feuding males, both men had managed to land scoring blows on the other.

'Mum, do something!' Angela demanded, wincing as Mitch settled a heavy punch into the younger man's stomach.

'Me? You're the one who brought him back here!' Vanessa snapped, angry with her daughter because she hadn't anticipated what would happen, and with herself because she hadn't thought to warn her anyway. God knew she'd been through this scene before too.

Just then Craig connected with a savage blow to Mitch's jaw which caused blood to dribble from his mouth.

'Stop! Stop!' Angela wailed as Mitch swung his foot and took Craig's legs out from under him and both men continued to wrestle in the dirt.

Vanessa swore, realising that, unless she did something, Angela would end up hysterical. Personally, as far as she was concerned the two of them could go at it until they both dropped from exhaustion.

She hurried down the steps and, taking care to give the writhing men a wide berth, ran to the far end of the house. Refusing to acknowledge the twinge of pride she felt as Mitch cuffed a telling blow on the chin of his much younger opponent, she picked up the heavy irrigation hose connected to the main water tank, turned the release valve and aimed a stream of water at the two brawling males.

CHAPTER TWO

'OUCH!'

Mitch pulled away at the first touch of the cotton ball against his grazed shoulder.

'Look, you asked me to do this! Now sit still so I can!' Vanessa ordered, not happy at having to play nurse to Mitch, who was naked from the waist up and looking so damned sexy she could feel her body temperature rising three degrees with each breath he took.

Ignoring her command, he pulled the first-aid kit closer and started to hunt through it.

'There should be some of that red stuff that doesn't sting...'

'Mercurochrome,' she said, watching his huge tanned hands searching the contents of the medicine kit and trying to forget how they'd felt moving over her body.

'Yeah. There should be a bottle of it in here. It's the last one I've got; it's almost impossible to find a chemist who'll sell the stuff since some fool scientist decided that because it had mercury in it it was poisonous!'

'I wish I'd known that earlier,' she muttered. 'This antiseptic would have been my second choice.'

'Cute, Vanessa. *Where the hell is it*?' Mitch continued to squirm from her touch.

'Angie took it over to Craig,' she responded, waving the cotton ball to indicate he should turn around so she could continue. All she wanted was to finish the job and have him clothe himself as quickly as possible.

'Damn. It's my first-aid kit; why should he get the Mercurochrome?'

How ironic that a grown man who not twenty minutes ago had initiated a brawl should be such a wimp when it came to iodine.

'Angie thought he was in worse shape than you were.'

'Huh! At my age I'll ache for a whole lot longer,' he grumbled.

'You should have thought of that before you went into your Mohammad Ali routine.'

'He had it coming.'

'Perhaps, but all you succeeded in doing was to elevate him to white knight status in Angie's eyes.'

'What the devil are you rabbiting on about, Vanessa?' he asked in an exasperated voice.

'I'm saying that, thanks to your "big tough father" routine, Angie sees Craig and herself as a modern-day Romeo and Juliet. There, your shoulder is finished.'

'Ta. Can you get an ice-pack from the fridge for me?' Mitch asked, gingerly feeling his face. 'My jaw is killing me.'

'While I have no hesitation in saying that your face looks a mess,' she said, pulling an ice-pack from the freezer and tossing it to him, 'don't expect me to sympathise.'

'Hell, no, Vanessa,' he said in pathetically righteous tone. 'The last thing I'd expect from you would be anything as unselfish as sympathy.' He shook his head. 'You haven't changed a bit.'

'At least I've grown up enough to know that fighting doesn't solve anything. Problems need to be talked out.' She walked to the window to put some distance between them.

'Does that mean that when things get too much for you these days you at least have the decency to say goodbye before you cut and run?' he retorted.

'Look, Mitch, I don't want to get into a discussion about the past—'

'Well, that's too bloody bad, because I do!' he said venomously. 'I want to know why you just upped and left without so much as a note! I want to know what the hell you thought you were doing not even giving me the chance to say goodbye to my daughter, and why you didn't even bother to contact me for three months to let me know she was OK? Do you have any idea what I went through those three months? Do you?'

'I…it wasn't easy for me either, Mitch.'

'Wasn't it? Well, *good*. I'm glad! I hope you went through every bit of pain that I did and then some! Because you deserved it; I didn't! At least if you suffered it was from choice.'

'Mitch, I…I…'

'You what? Don't want to discuss it? Now why doesn't that surprise me? One minute you're saying you've grown up and the next you're shying away from something you find unpleasant, just as you did ten years ago. Just as you've always done. Your motto has always been, if things get tense—get out! You can't stomach confrontations so you just avoid them.'

'That's not fair!'

'Neither was the way you ended our marriage!'

'Our marriage was over long before I left Brayburn and you know it!'

'Did you ever once think that as Angela's father I was entitled to at least be told face to face of your plans?'

'How? You were never home longer than it took to get a change of clothes and eat a meal. And even then you barely spoke to me.'

'That's crap! I was home plenty! But any time I tried to engage you in conversation you'd tell me you had to study, or you had an essay to write, or you had to bath Angela, or you had to colour-code your sock drawer!'

'Look, I'm not up to this—'

'Right! Let's not have a discussion that you don't want to have…'

'Oh, for God's sake, Mitch, give me a break! I'm tired, I've flown clear across the country and I'm having a tough enough time dealing with my current problems to worry about past ones!' To her own ears her words had a slightly pleading ring; she only hoped Mitch hadn't detected the same weakness of tone.

Yet when she looked at him, there were so many conflicting emotions flashing across his face and in his eyes—dejection, surprise, regret, hope, uncertainty—that it was impossible to ascertain what he was thinking.

'I need some air!' he said viciously, striding to the door as if she had actually refused to let him breathe.

As soon as he'd gone Vanessa slumped on to the closest chair and tried to relax. Her hands were trembling. *In... out...in...out...* She commanded herself to take deep, steadying breaths.

'Oh, lord,' she practically panted the address. 'Please get me through these next few days. *Just let me get through them.*'

Dinner started as a disaster and went downhill from there.

'Angela, honey, what's the matter?' Vanessa's concerned words were prompted by the tears that were streaming down her daughter's face. Her query drew Mitch from the silence he'd practised since they'd first sat down fifteen minutes ago.

'Baby, what is it?' he asked, reaching for the teenager's hand. Angela snatched it away.

'I th-think Craig's nose is...is broken.' she sobbed.

'Aw, baby...' Vanessa saw her ex-husband struggle to turn a satisfied smirk into a reassuring smile. 'That's nothing. Craig's nose has been broken lots of times.'

'It's your fault!' Angela accused her father. 'You had no reason to act like a...a...crazed lunatic! You could have killed him!'

'I've got the best reason in the world! He's been sleeping with my daughter and now she's pregnant! If I'd had the slightest idea what was going on I'd have killed him four months ago!'

'Mitch!' Vanessa's shout was drowned out by Angela's wails and the crash of her chair hitting the ground as the girl raced from the room. 'Angie, wait!'

'Angela!' Mitch yelled, moving from his chair to follow.

'Sit down, Mitch,' Vanessa ordered. 'I think you've done and said enough today, don't you?'

Docile obedience was something Mitch had never been familiar with and Vanessa couldn't say whether she was more pleased or shocked when she returned to the dining-room thirty minutes later to discover him sitting exactly where she'd left him. He was so deep in thought that he physically started as she approached the table. She wondered where his thoughts had been and almost voiced the question before common sense gave her curiosity a good kick.

It wasn't her place to demand access to his private thoughts any more. Even when it had been Mitch had locked her out.

'How is she?' he asked impatiently.

'She's calmed down some,' she told him. 'And she wants to talk to you.'

'Thank God for that much,' Mitch muttered.

Regardless of what had transpired during and since their marriage, Vanessa realised that Mitch had always been a good father to Angela. For that reason many people would have thought what she had to say was unnecessary, but from personal experience she knew otherwise.

'Before you talk to her there are a few things I want to say.'

She met his eyes and as he moistened his lips in preparation for the cigarette he held only inches from them, Vanessa was hit with an onslaught of desire so fierce her legs nearly buckled beneath her. Even after all these years her body still reacted to him as it never had with any other man. Not that she'd ever been game enough to chance either her heart or her body to anyone since Mitch. Maybe this sudden onslaught of sensuality was the result of the imminent approach of her thirty-fifth birthday and almost eleven years of celibacy? Ludicrous as the notion was, it was preferable to crediting Mitch Randall as the cause.

'What is it you want to say, Vanessa?'

The way he drew her name out with deliberate slowness so, like he used to do when in the throes of passion made her fear he'd read her mind. But when she searched his face it was unreadable, and the sight of him striking a match was a bitter reminder of the more tragic aspects of her marriage. She steeled herself against the lick of pain that tore through her as Mitch drew heavily on the end of his cigarette.

Twelve years ago, when she'd learned she was pregnant for a second time, she'd jokingly told Mitch that if he gave up smoking she'd make sure the baby was a boy. He'd laughed, but from that moment on he'd ceased to smoke, though he'd often tease her by saying that if it was a girl he'd seriously have to consider resuming the tobacco addiction, since living in a house with three women would be havoc on any man's nerves. Yet it hadn't been the birth of a second daughter which had prompted Mitch to revert to his old habit. It had been the death of their unborn son. The tragedy had destroyed them.

'Vanessa?'

His voice shattered her memories and she became aware that she was crumbling the crust of what remained of her now cold pizza into dust. She pushed the plate away and forced herself to concentrate one what had to be said.

'As much as I would give anything to be able to wake up and find these last few days have been nothing more than a bizarre nightmare, I know that's not going to happen.' She paused and looked at Mitch.

'No,' he agreed. 'Unfortunately this is reality.'

Vanessa shook her head and sighed. 'No, worse than that. To me it's been like a slow-motion replay of what happened to us.' She took a determined breath and pinned him with a hard glance before continuing. 'But this is where it stops. I don't want to watch my daughter go through what I did. I don't want her to feel her parents are ashamed or disappointed in her behaviour—'

'Now just a minute!' Mitch cut in. 'If you're implying I'm ashamed of Angela because—'

'No! That's not what I'm saying. But I don't want her to even have reason to *think* we might be. I've been in her shoes, Mitch, and I know how my father—'

'Don't ever equate me with your father, Vanessa.' Mitch's warning was menacingly soft. 'I love Angela and nothing she does is ever going to change that.'

She knew what he said was the truth and for a split-second she was envious of her own child. Ashamed of the thought, she pushed it away.

'She needs to hear that from you, Mitch. She needs to be reassured that we both love her and that we'll always be supportive of her and the baby.'

'And the baby? She's decided to keep it?'

Vanessa nodded. 'She told me that regardless of how either of us felt about it she had no intention of giving it up.'

'I'd say that, like me, you didn't have any doubts she would,' he said.

'No. Not really.'

His wry smile warmed her all over. She wondered if she was strong enough to endure three days in this man's presence and ignore, or at best resist, the pull of his magnetism. Despite all the assurances she'd given herself that time would have eroded the attraction she felt for Mitch, nothing had changed. At fifteen, one look from her father's brash young stockman had knocked the breath from her lungs—and almost twenty years later she still couldn't breathe.

She felt herself blush and self-consciously ran one hand from her temple to the ends of her hair. He stared at her as if mesmerised by the action and the air seemed charged by the electricity in his gaze.

'Your hair has always reminded me of sunlight bouncing off copper. I like it long.'

His words were so unexpected that Vanessa was powerless to respond.

'You look good.'

She gave a dry laugh. 'Emotionally I feel as if I've been hit by a truck.'

'Me too.'

The tone of his voice caused her head to jerk up. She'd been referring to finding out Angie's condition, but she was sure he didn't mean the same thing. Her heart was pounding as she met his gaze.

To her his eyes were synonymous with the Australian sky: the purest of blues when he was in a sunny mood and a stormy grey-navy when he was angry. In passion they were hot enough to melt her bones and in anger they immobilised with just a glance. There had been a time when she'd never believed she'd ever be on the receiving end of Mitch's angry glare, but in the final year of their marriage she'd fallen prey to it many times. Yet ultimately it had been the lifeless look of heartbreak, disappointment and most often accusation in those eyes that had forced her to leave Brayburn. The painful memories made her look away.

'So,' Mitch said. 'How's your mother?'

Mitch had never been a big fan of her mother's so the topic, as much as the tone, told her he was as anxious as she to dispel the emotion in the air.

'Fine. I haven't told her the news yet.'

'Who's she married to currently?' he enquired snidely. 'Last I heard it was some retired lawyer from Sydney. What was his name?'

'Patrick Willis. They're still together.'

'Struth! That must be what…nearly four years? She must be approaching her record.'

'Mother's longest marriage lasted nine years,' she told him rising to her feet. 'It was to my father.'

'That long, huh?' he said with pseudo awe.

'You shouldn't be so smug, Mitch. Your track record isn't even *that* good!'

'I wasn't the one who bailed out, Vanessa,' he reminded her harshly.

'I didn't *bail out*. I was pushed!'

She didn't dare look at him so she began collecting the dinner dishes, trying hard not to chink them against one another. She was less than steady under Mitch's piercing gaze.

'Leave them, Vanessa. Cora can do them in the morning.'

'No…I'll do them.'

There were so many old grievances on the tip of her tongue that she clamped it between her teeth to stop any escaping. Lord, how was it possible for one man to push her to the brink of so many conflicting emotions in such a short space of time? Her hands continued to tremble and the rattle of china seemed to fill the whole room.

'For God's sake, leave them!'

At Mitch's sudden command she dropped the stacked plates back on to the table. Several shattered.

'Oh, no! I'm sor-sorry. I…I…'

Mitch swore and jumped to his feet.

'I'm sorry,' she repeated, intimidated as much by his nearness as his barely controlled anger. He looked like fury served straight up with a touch of ice for good measure. Why he had such an affection for a cheap dinner service was beyond her, but then pretty much everything was beyond her right now. 'I'll buy a new set, OK?'

'For God's sake, forget the dishes! The dishes don't matter.'

He pulled her into his arms and held her against his chest as he soothingly stroked her hair. His strength reminded her of all she'd missed and still longed for and his gentleness broke her heart. She couldn't let herself get caught up in old emotions. Where she and Mitch were concerned it wasn't just a case of too much water having gone over the dam, but rather a case of the dam being totally destroyed in the process. The debris left from their stormy relationship could never be cleared away. Nor could the mortality rate.

Vanessa felt her soul rip in two and with a shuddering wail she succumbed to her emotions.

Secure in Mitch's arms, she allowed herself to be lulled by the soothing rhythm of his hand stroking her back. She closed her eyes and in her mind the years ebbed back to that time in their life when their biggest worry was whether Mitch would have time to take a long lunch-break and return to the house to make love with her. Miraculously, when she lifted her lids she imagined she saw a three-year-old Angela standing at the foot of the stairs holding her stuffed panda. Her happiness was exquisite.

'Mum?'

She blinked and ruined everything.

'Dad? Is Mum OK?' Angela left the stairs and moved into the room.

'Sure, honey, I'm fine.' Vanessa forced a bright smile at her daughter as she pushed herself free of Mitch. 'Just a bit upset because I broke your dad's dinner set.'

'Oh.' The teenager looked from one parent to the other. 'Well, I just came down to say goodnight and to show you what I found in the attic. Look, Panda Poo!'

Vanessa looked at the bedraggled black and white toy.

'Why on earth would you dig that old thing up?'

'So I can pass it on to my baby, of course!' came the laughing reply. 'I'm really going to get into that attic tomorrow. You wouldn't believe the stuff that's up there!' She kissed both her parents goodnight and returned to the stairs. 'Even my old crib is still up there. It's an absolute treasure-trove! Well, goodnight!'

'Goodnight, honey,' Vanessa said, grateful her daughter hadn't made any sarcastic comments about finding her parents in one another's arms.

'Hey, Angie,' Mitch called after her. 'OK if I come up and have a chat with you?'

'Sure, Dad. You know, I think I'll sleep with Panda Poo tonight,' she laughed. 'I used to love snuggling up to him.'

'I wish she'd remembered that last July!' Vanessa complained. 'It might have kept her from improvising with Craig.'

Mitch arched his eyebrows. 'You think a stuffed toy would have kept you satisfied at eighteen? Because if so I have a dozen recollections that will correct that misconception.'

With that he turned on his heel and followed his daughter upstairs, leaving her with her heart slamming against her ribs.

Vanessa sat down in front of the mirror and unscrewed the lid of her eye make-up remover. What a day! She was so wiped out that if she'd been a residential area, the government would have declared her a disaster area and TV networks would be organising a telethon to raise funds for reconstruction!

She dipped a cotton ball into the jar of bilious green goop and smeared it over her face, wishing she could just fall into bed make-up and all, but with her thirty-fifth birthday just around the corner she wasn't taking any chances. Not that she was vain, but these days she did believe in making the best of her appearance.

Ten years ago her idea of daily make-up had been cold cream, moisturiser and sunscreen. Lipstick had been an indulgence for social occasions. After she left Brayburn she'd had to rebuild her life and a beauty and deportment course had been her first step. Step two had been to use the private trust fund set up by her late grandparents to open an exclusive clothing boutique specialising in creations from the best

Australian and international designers. These days she considered that her personal appearance was an advertisement for her business, and she couldn't afford to let herself get sloppy.

She moved closer to the mirror and massaged the fine lines at the corner of her eyes. Her mother always said a few lines added character to a woman's face. She smiled. Perhaps Mitch thought the same, she mused, recalling his comment that she 'looked good'. The smile turned to a scowl. It shouldn't matter to her what Mitch thought!

Angry with herself, she ignored the recommended gentle strokes and scrubbed hard at the resilient eyeshadow until it was all off. She was no gentler with her cleanser, but she figured she deserved the self-flagellation.

'God, how did my life get so complicated again in just a few days?' She sighed, half wishing she knew what tomorrow would bring yet simultaneously hoping it would never come.

After completing her tedious nightly ritual with an application of moisturiser, Vanessa picked up her brush and gave her hair a few quick strokes. Yet, when she stopped, static electricity continued to draw her hair to the bristles. In the mirror she watched as the bronze strands fell back into place in slow motion.

Your hair has always reminded me of sunlight bouncing off copper...

Vanessa swore. 'Eeeeehh! Get out of my head, Mitch Randall!'

She snatched up ribbon and viciously pulled her hair into a ponytail at the back of her neck.

I'm just overtired, she told herself as she climbed into bed. All I need is a good night's sleep and I'll be back to my old self. No! My *usual* self, she amended. The old Vanessa would never be able to cope with the current situation.

At two-fifteen a.m. Vanessa couldn't have been more awake if someone had thrown a bucket of cold water over her. She only wished someone would! Very cold water!

She was shocked by the intense physical attraction Mitch still stirred within her. Surely after ten years it should have lessened, not intensified! At nearly thirty-five, she wasn't sure she should be experiencing the torrent of conflicting emotions raging within her. She could barely keep her eyes off him, and just the thought of his touch was increasing her heart-rate and causing tingling sensations deep inside her. Despite her celibate life since leaving him, Vanessa had mentally replayed Mitch's lovemaking techniques enough times to be able to identify the demands of her own sexual appetite. Except this time she was sure a mental replay wasn't likely to satisfy them.

Great! she thought, I'm about to become a nanna and my body is tempting my mind with things that would make a hooker blush!

Getting out of bed, she slipped on a satin teddy and ankle length robe. Then she fished the carton of camomile tea she'd packed out of her suitcase. She needed something soothing. Unfortunately fate served up just the opposite…

'Yet another one who can't sleep.'

The unexpected sound of Mitch's voice caused her to slop hot tea over the rim of the cup she carried.

'Owww! Lord, Mitch, you scared me half to death!'

'Sorry.'

He was propped against the timber railing at the far end of the veranda, a dark silhouette against the even darker backdrop of the night.

'I made myself some herbal tea,' she said, pleased to find her voice sounded normal. 'I didn't know you were out here or I'd have made you one too.'

'You didn't know I was here or you wouldn't have come out, you mean.' He laughed. 'Herbal tea, Vanessa? Don't tell me you've gone all trendy and health-conscious.'

'It happens to be very relaxing. It helps me sleep.'

'You have trouble sleeping?' He sounded concerned.

'Not usually,' she replied, sitting down in a wicker chair that was a safe twenty feet from him and bathed in the soft light coming from the kitchen. 'But the last few days have been far from usual.'

His face was momentarily illuminated by the match he carried to his cigarette and the hard planes of his handsomeness appeared vulnerable in the flickering light. Yet when the match was extinguished his voice conveyed no sign of vulnerability.

'What happens now, Vanessa?'

'What do you mean?'

'I mean, what are your plans now Angie's decided to keep the baby? Now that you and I have presented a united front of support for her? What is the next game play, as you would call it?'

He sounded challenging and a touch smug. As if he knew more than she did and was waiting for her to give the wrong response so he could correct her.

'Well, the most important thing is to get Angela under the care of a good obstetrician. I've already spoken to my gynaecologist in Perth; she doesn't practice obstetrics, so she's referred Angie to a colleague who's regarded as the best in the state. Naturally I'll leave the choice of hospital up to him.'

The creak of the veranda's aged timber floor came only a millionth of a second before the increase in Vanessa's pulserate to warn her of Mitch's approach.

He positioned himself on the rail directly in front of her; his back against the upright supporting the roof, one leg bent to provide a rest for his arm and the other touching the ground to counter-balance his weight on the narrow rail. She took a hearty sip of her tea, but decided the drink's pacifying qualities weren't all they were cracked up to be.

'Of course, there are hundreds of minor things to be considered,' she continued, refusing to be sidetracked by the concentrated male sexuality Mitch dispensed via his body and nonchalant pose. 'I haven't really decided whether I'll keep my unit or sell it and buy a house.'

'What's where you live got to do with anything?'

'Well, the unit might be fine while the baby is small, but it'll need a yard to play in once it gets older.'

'You intend for Angie to live with you?'

'Of course,' she said. 'You can't seriously believe I'd force her to find somewhere else to live, do you?'

'What if she wanted to?'

'What? Don't be ridiculous, Mitch—even if Angie could afford to get her own place, she's not going to be able to meet the cost of child care and food. Now she's been forced to defer a year of her uni course, it's going to be at least another four until she has her degree and is employable.'

'So you plan to let Angie and the baby stay with you and you'll pick up the childcare tab until Angie finishes university?'

'Yes. I can afford it. Although Angie said tonight that Craig was insistent about facing his responsibilities. Noble, but hardly a guarantee of financial security.'

'She say anything else about Craig?'

'I think she stopped short of claiming he could walk on water, but I'm not sure. For peace of mind I try and tune out when she mentions his name.'

'Maybe it's about time you stopped considering yourself and listened to what your daughter wants.'

'Stop thinking of *myself*!' Vanessa was outraged. How dared he imply she didn't care about Angie's feelings?

'OK, calm down. I worded that badly,' Mitch conceded. 'What I meant to say is perhaps it's time you started to *really* listen to what Angela is saying.'

Vanessa watched as he studied the tip of his cigarette before continuing. Despite the warmth of the night a sharp chill climbed over her.

'When I spoke to her earlier,' he said slowly, 'I got the distinct impression that returning to Perth isn't on her agenda.'

'Don't be ridiculous! She knows she has an appointment with the obstetrician in four days time.'

'He's not the only one in the country, Vanessa,' Mitch pointed out, but gave her no time to respond. 'Anyway, after talking with Angie I went down to see O'Brien.'

'Was he at least conscious when you left him?'

The diffused light from within the house momentarily bounced off Mitch's perfect teeth as he smiled at her comment.

'I *talked* with the kid, Vanessa. Nothing more.' He paused as if trying to formulate how best to continue.

'And?'

'And,' Mitch sighed, 'he wants to marry her.'

Cold dread washed over Vanessa like a tidal wave and her stomach churned in response. No! her heart screamed. Not again!

CHAPTER THREE

VANESSA could feel the weight of Mitch's eyes watching her, but it was several moments before she was capable of producing a rational response.

'I hope you rammed home the absurdity of that as a solution,' she said, determined to remain calm.

'I started to.' He paused and stood up. 'Then I realised that he feels exactly the same way about Angie as she does about him.'

'She's *infatuated* with him, Mitch. Nothing more! Angie has a teenage crush on Craig that's no different from the ones she's had on dozens of other boys since she started high school!'

'I don't think so,' Mitch stated with soft certainty. 'Angie loves Craig...'

'No!' Vanessa jumped to her feet as she voiced the denial. 'She's *in love* with him. There's a big difference! And she's not going to marry him! We won't let her!'

'We can't stop her,' Mitch said softly, his face gentle as he looked down over the nine-inch difference in their heights. 'She's eighteen. And she's made up her mind.'

Every organ in Vanessa's body began to ice over. He was going to back Angie. Mitch was going to give his blessing to a marriage any thinking person could see was doomed! He was going to let two kids risk getting ensnared in exactly the same trap they had.

She pushed past him and ran to the end of the veranda. Tears were washing down her face and her lungs were burning for air. She gripped the railing and squeezed it until the pain in her hands distracted her from the pain of her past.

'Vanes—'

'Don't touch me!' She shrugged away the hand Mitch had placed on her back, but swung around to face him. 'You're going to agree to this…this…' she could barely get the word out '…this *marriage*, aren't you?'

'My agreement is inconsequential. All I want is Angie's happiness.'

'So do I!' Vanessa said. 'But, unlike you, I'm thinking long-term. She hardly knows this guy! He's—'

'Craig's a good kid.'

'That's not what you were saying a few hours ago, Mitch. *Then* you painted him as a cross between the devil himself and Charles Manson and were ready to punch him to a pulp.'

'Most fathers would have reacted the same way. I was shocked and upset,' he said, rolling his broad masculine shoulders in a futile attempt to portray helplessness. 'At times I still see Angela as my little girl instead of my grown daughter.'

'She's still too young to get married. She's only eighteen.'

'She's two years older than you were when you married me and Craig's twenty-one, three years older than I was.'

'I'm well aware of how old you and I were, Mitch, but this is different.'

'How?'

'For starters I'd known you since I was fifteen. Angie met Craig less than six months ago and until today hasn't even seen him for nearly five! That hardly compares with our situation.'

'If they love one another I don't see that as being relevant.'

'Oh, for God's sake, Mitch! What about Angie's degree? She's a bright girl with her whole future to consider. It didn't matter with me; I was only ever an average student.'

Mitch's hearty chuckle filled the night. 'I'm not sure

whether that was a back-handed compliment or an insult, Nessa!'

The use of his pet name for her caused her mind to short-circuit and for a few seconds she was hard pressed to remember what she'd been saying. Yet, as she picked up her train of thought, much of the anger she'd been feeling had dissipated.

'The fact is, Angie has a good brain—'

'OK,' he said generously. 'Since you happily admit to being no great loss to the academic world, I'll take the genetic credit for that.'

'This isn't funny, Mitch!' she said, in a desperate bid to keep her mouth from curling. 'Angie deserves a chance to make something of herself before she gets tied down to marriage with someone who spends every daylight hour with cows, bulls and horses and every spare hour after that planning for more cows, more bulls and more horses!'

'I did not spend every spare hour planning "more cows, more bulls and more horses"!' Mitch mimicked as he moved towards her.

'Hah! You always did have a poor memory, but senility is making it worse!' she accused, before realising she was personalising the issue. 'But this isn't about us.'

'Isn't it?' he countered, dangerously softly, his eyes roaming over her face with obvious hunger. 'Didn't *you* liken the current situation between Angie and Craig to a slow-motion replay of our relationship?'

Vanessa could feel herself being enmeshed in the web of sensuality that his seductive drawl was spinning in the darkness. She moved in a desperate bid to reach the kitchen door, but Mitch blocked her way. A work-calloused hand reached beneath her hair and lilted her face towards him. Mesmerised, she didn't move as he traced a finger along her jaw.

'Ah, Nessa, where you're concerned I have a perfect memory. Everything about you stayed with me. The copper glow of your hair, the sound of your laugh and especially the way your eyes turn from the colour of whisky to almost black when you're making love.'

She closed her eyes as a final defence against his assault on her senses. But closed eyes were futile against Mitch's deliberately slow stroking of her cheeks.

'You have skin like satin, Nessa,' he whispered with reverence. 'Know how many times I've pushed the rewind button in my mind and replayed different scenes of us, so I could recall the feel of your skin?'

'M-Mitch, please...'

'Remember the time we took off to the dam for an afternoon of lovemaking, when I should have been overseeing the branding?'

Her traitorous mind zoomed straight to the random memory he drew upon and a tiny spark in her abdomen threatened to blaze through her body. She willed herself to push him aside and walk away, but her legs would have no part of it. Nor could she withhold the sigh or the reaction of her nipples as he moved his hands to her breast.

'Don't...Mitch...'

'I can also recall in glorious detail the night we made love in the downstairs bathroom, while the largest stock and station agent in the state sat in the library waiting for me to discuss the purchase of a prize stud bull.'

Her eyes flew open in amazement. The same incident had just sprung to her own mind!

He gave a slow smile. 'The irony of the situation has only dawned in retrospect.'

As his mouth drew nearer, her common sense implored her to act on her brain's screams to flee, but her body wouldn't co-operate. It was being tempted by recollections of how good Mitch Randall had tasted and a curiosity to see if the flavour of his lovemaking was just as exotic now.

When his tongue lightly touched the corner of her mouth, Vanessa's blood turned to steam; she could no more have kept her lips sealed to him than flown. Her heart pounded until it deafened her, his tongue tangled her own beyond speech and she was left with only three functioning senses: her taste, which was being swamped by the uniquely sensual flavour of Mitch after years of being denied; her sense of smell, which failed to register anything but the earthy masculine scent of the man who held her and the heady aroma of their arousal; and finally her sense of touch, which was too confused by the feel of Mitch's rough male jaw against her neck and the softness of his hair between her fingers to decide which felt better.

Time and again they ravaged each other's mouths until the need to breathe forced them to stop and draw deep, ragged breaths. Vanessa took consolation, for the absence of Mitch's mouth against her own, from the sensations his hands were creating as they panned over her hips and buttocks with familiar warmth and desire.

'God, Nessa, it hasn't changed. There's still more heat between us than there is in hell,' Mitch muttered against her neck before he lifted his head to look at her. 'Let's go inside.'

His words jarred. There had been times during their marriage when a trip to hell would have seemed like a vacation in Disneyland! Despite what her body was telling her, she wasn't ready for this. She didn't *want* it! Physically maybe, but emotionally *no*.

Her legs were less than steady and her breathing no better, but her resolve was set in concrete and when Mitch bent to scoop her into his arms she pushed at him and moved swiftly out of reach. Taking advantage of his surprise, she retreated into the kitchen and locked the screen door.

'Vanessa?'

'Things *have* changed, Mitch. Especially me. And as for those romantic little interludes you mentioned—on reflection you'll notice they only serve to prove our relationship was squeezed in around your precious cattle!'

His denial took the form of a succinct one-word response as he shook the handle of the door.

She figured the flimsy catch would last about two minutes. She was halfway down the hall when he called after her.

'Hell, Nessa, since when have you objected to a good squeeze?'

Vanessa began trying to get her daughter to see reason the minute the teenagers arrived at the breakfast table.

'Angie, I realise why you might feel obliged to marry Craig, but it's hardly necessary in this day and age.'

'I don't feel *obliged* to marry him, Mum. I *want* to marry him,' Angela corrected. 'I love Craig.'

'But don't you think it would be wiser to wait and see whether this love will endure before you forgo your education?'

'Mum! You said whatever I decided to do you'd go along with it.'

'I meant regarding whether you kept the baby or had it adopted.' Self-consciously Vanessa glanced at the rotund housekeeper. Satisfied the woman didn't appear interested in what was being discussed, she continued, 'I never expected you would want to toss your entire future away!'

'Calm down, Vanessa,' Mitch cautioned with concerned eyes. 'Take it easy.'

'Take it easy!' she retorted. 'Would you mind telling me just how the hell you expect Craig to support a wife and child?' she demanded, her gaze including both father and daughter. 'My God, he lives in the stockmen's quarters! What are you planning to do, Angela? Pitch a tent down by the dam and set up house there?'

It was Mitch who responded to her question.

'I've told Angie and Craig they can live in the old home-stead house until they get things sorted out. Your father did as much for us.'

'Mitch! How could you?' She felt as if she'd been kicked. 'That's where all our problems started! Don't you realise that?'

'That's rubbish, Vanessa!'

'Mum, just because you and Dad messed things up, it doesn't mean Craig and I will. It's not fair to judge us by what happened to you.'

'*Not fair*? Angela, I am only trying to make you open your eyes to what can happen. Sure, my father helped Mitch and me out, but at what cost to us? He put so much damned pressure on our marriage it's a miracle it lasted beyond your first birthday, let alone eight years!'

Out of the corner of her eye Vanessa saw Mitch's mouth narrow, but she ignored him. He'd done enough damage as it was! She hurried on before he could do any more.

'At first I was thrilled when Daddy announced he wanted to help us. But by God, I've regretted it ever since!'

'But that's *you*, Mum, not *me*,' Angela argued. 'Craig's and my marriage isn't going to be something I regret. I *know* it will last.'

'Angie, I felt the same about my marriage when I was your age. But I grew up and woke up! It's all very well to have twenty-twenty vision in hindsight, but it's not worth a damn!'

'Mum, I'm *in love* with Craig. Why can't you understand that?'

'I do understand it, but being in love isn't enough.'

'It is for me! You're just angry because Daddy wants to help us and that means the baby will be living here, not with you!'

'Angie!' Vanessa gasped. The look on Mitch's face suggested he thought Angela had raised a valid point. Hurting beyond belief, she could only stammer a denial. 'That's... that's not true.'

'Sorry, Mum, but I've spent enough time living among

smog and pollution when I've only ever wanted to be here at Brayburn. I'm not—'

'You...you...*never* said you wanted to live here.' Vanessa almost physically reeled as another wave of shock hit her before the last had managed to stop vibrating through her nervous system.

'You never asked.' Angela shrugged. 'Dad knew, but he said it'd hurt you too much if I told you I wanted to live here. Well, now I have someone else's feelings I have to consider.'

'Angie...' Vanessa's mind was a fog and she was struggling to find the right words. 'Angie, you don't have to marry Craig just because you want to stay here. We—'

'I love Craig and I'm going to marry him. If you can't accept that, Mum, then fine! But don't hold up what happened to your marriage and tell me mine is doomed! Unlike you, I intend to at least *try* and make mine work!'

'That's enough, Angela!' Mitch said.

'Dad, why are you taking her side...?'

Unable to bear any more, Vanessa ran from the house...

It wasn't until the horse beneath her was wet with sweat that Vanessa realised the enormity of what she'd just done. She didn't know whether to laugh or cry.

Instinctively she slowed the horse to a walk and released the vicelike grip she held on her mane. Everyone knew that if you fell off a horse the first thing you had to do was dust yourself down and get right back on. Except the last time Vanessa had fallen from a horse, she'd woken up in a hospital with a crushed pelvis, a broken leg and devoid of the son she'd carried in her womb for seven months. Getting back on hadn't been an option and she'd never ridden since.

That she was sitting bareback astride a mount she'd never seen before was proof of reactive behaviour, not the deliberate action she'd been advised to take by the shrink who'd been called in to counsel her after the accident. Not that she'd ever listened to him; the guy had been a jerk.

She made no attempt to wipe away the tears running down her face because in a strange way she felt they weren't coming from her eyes, but from her soul. In her mind she pictured the small family graveyard to the west of the house and sent a silent prayer up for her son.

Beneath her she felt the horse tense for a second before it quickened its stride and the action was enough to alert her to her surroundings. The creek which wound through almost two-thirds of the property was just beyond the rise.

'OK, girl,' she said, patting the mare's neck. 'I agree. I'm thirsty too.'

It wasn't until she'd slid from the animal's back, and it careened across to the other side of the creek, that Vanessa remembered that without a bridle the horse was unlikely to remain 'ground tied' even if she had been trained to it.

She swore at her own stupidity, before the drone of an engine broke the morning's peace. Turning she saw a trail-bike become airborne on the top of the rise, then bounce a couple of times after it hit the ground. She was beginning to have serious doubts about whether the 'rider from hell' intended to mow her down when she recognised him as Mitch. That didn't mean she was safe, but at least if she survived she'd know whose insurance company to sue!

When he was about twenty feet from her he killed the engine and vaulted from the bike, leaving it to topple sideways.

'Vanessa! Are you all right?'

She nodded, but his blue eyes were moving over her as if he needed to assure himself of the fact. Gradually his harried expression relaxed into relief.

'Thank God,' he murmured pulling her against him.

Her arms were trapped by her sides and her face was almost being crushed against his chest. He held her so fiercely that his shirt buttons would be bound to leave divots in her cheeks and his heart was pounding harder against her ribs than her own.

'Mitch.' She could only manage a croak. 'Mitch, let go, I can't breathe.' There was no weakening in the bear-hug restricting her. '*Mitch*!'

He released her so quickly that she staggered.

'Struth, Vanessa! Do that again and I'll purposely suffocate you!' he roared. 'Do you have any idea what I went through when Craig said he'd seen you riding like a bat out of hell from the horse yard?'

He looked livid as he paced back and forth in a one-metre area as if he were trapped in a gaol cell, instead of being in a paddock that stretched forever. But she knew exactly what he'd thought and guilt nibbled at her.

'I'm sorry.' An involuntary shiver went through her. 'I didn't realise what I was doing until I was practically here.'

'Is that suppose to make me feel *better*?'

'Look, if I'd been thinking straight I would never have jumped on any horse, let alone one I didn't know, but I wasn't! OK?' She softened her tone. 'I'm sorry I put you through a lot of bad memories, but I'm not hurt.'

He grunted in response and walked over to stand up the motorbike.

'How's Angie? Has she calmed down?' she asked.

'How would I know?' he said tersely. 'I raced out after you, expecting to find you on the veranda! When you weren't there I checked the machinery shed. I was about to head up to Samuel's grave when I ran into Craig.'

Samuel's grave. Vanessa's heart cramped up. Mitch always referred to their son by the name he'd posthumously been baptised by. She never did. It was he who'd chosen it. Although it had been Vanessa who had insisted on having a proper funeral for their son, the doctors had refused to let her out of hospital to attend it. Since then she'd mentally knelt in the small cemetery and prayed for the little boy she'd loved but never known a zillion times, yet she'd never had the strength to visit it physically. Had Mitch known this, he'd not have considered looking for her there.

'Vanessa, are you sure you're OK?'

Quickly she blinked away the mist of tears blurring her vision.

'Yeah, all I have to do now is figure out how to convince her.' She pointed across the creek to the horse idly chewing grass. 'To surrender her freedom and give me a ride back.'

'Don't bother, I'll take you back on the bike,' he told her. 'I'll send one of the blokes out to bring her in later.'

'If you always ride the way you did coming over that hill, then I'd just as soon walk.'

'I promise it will be a more sedate trip home.'

'Make sure it is,' she warned, moving to the vehicle.

'Wait!'

She stopped at the urgency in his voice and turned back to face him.

'I think this might be a good opportunity to discuss what happened at breakfast.'

She opened her mouth to refuse, but Mitch's determined expression made the words dry up. For a time their eyes argued the point back and forth. It was Vanessa who looked away first, knowing that, much as she wanted to, she couldn't avoid the inevitable.

She knew Mitch had smelt his victory when he sat down and propped his back against the peeling bark of a silver gum.

'So what do you want to discuss first?' Her tone was deliberately challenging. 'My selfish motives for not wanting to see my daughter ruin her life? My neurotic wish to provide her and the baby with a safe comfortable home until they are financially self-sufficient? Or the possibility that I harbour a secret relish to see my child unhappy?'

'You through with the sarcasm?' Mitch asked. 'If not, we'll discuss this when you're in a more reasonable frame of mind.'

She reefed at a long tuft of weed. She had to start accepting the fact that she was on the wrong team in a three-against-one match. She didn't have to like the final score line, but she had to accept it.

'I realise Angie is eighteen and doesn't legally need our permission to marry, Mitch.' As she spoke she concentrated on a solitary cloud floating in the otherwise totally blue sky. She identified with the cloud's loneliness. 'But I can't understand why you're so eager to aid and abet her in something that I think amounts to emotional suicide.'

'She's my daughter,' he said simply.

'She's also mine.'

There was no further conversation for some minutes. It was Mitch who initiated it.

'I love Angie, but I've never aspired to see her as anything more than happy. I know she's smart,' he said quickly as if fearing Vanessa would interrupt him to point this out. 'But there are plenty of smart people about who are never happy. More than anything I want Angie to be happy.'

'And you're certain she'll find it married to Craig O'Brien?' Vanessa couldn't conceal her scepticism.

'I can't say I don't have reservations about her rushing into marriage, in fact I even amazed myself by suggesting she and Craig live together for a while. But I know when I'm fighting a losing battle.'

'But the battle mightn't have been lost if we'd combined forces! Can't you see that!'

'No. I'm not sure our motives for wanting to win are the same.'

His gaze was fixed on the horizon of grassed hills, but Vanessa didn't need to see the accusation in his eyes. It had come across loud and clear in his tone.

'You think I only want Angie in Perth so I can raise her baby as my own, don't you?'

She got no response. God, did he really believe she was that selfish? Was his opinion of her so low he'd interpreted her

genuine concern for her daughter's future as nothing more than
an act?

Surely in view of his stance she had just as much right to
suspect his motives? But she hadn't. Had she? No! It was too
bizarre to imagine Mitch would resort to punishing her for the
loss of his son by ensuring she'd have only limited contact
with her grandchild. Desperately she shoved the notion aside
before it took root in her mind, and asked the question which
bothered her the most.

'Why didn't you tell me that Angie wasn't happy living
with me in Perth?'

Mitch stood up and walked to the edge of the creek before
answering.

'Because I knew you loved her…and I thought you needed
her more than I did.' He turned and nailed her with a hard
glare. 'So did you, otherwise you'd not have taken her with
you when you walked out, knowing how much she loved this
place.'

'She was eight years old! No woman could leave a child
that young!'

'Your mother did.'

Vanessa couldn't deny the truth. In fact she'd been only
three when her father had granted his wife her freedom in
exchange for uncontested custody of their daughter. How different her life might have been, from the years of nannies and
boarding schools, had her mother valued Vanessa's happiness
over her pride.

Was *that* what *she* was doing now? Placing her own private
fears above *her* daughter's possible happiness? She'd only
ever wanted to protect Angela from unnecessary pain and to
see her happy. But now they held conflicting opinions over
which path would lead to that often elusive state of mind.
Angie favoured the scenic cliffside route, which Vanessa knew
was narrow and almost impossible to negotiate because one
slip could plunge you into the sea of heartbreak. As a mother

Vanessa wanted Angie to continue along the less exciting but much safer path she was currently travelling.

She shook her head to dispel the inane analogy she painted in her mind. As usual she was being fanciful instead of realistic.

She looked at Mitch, now sitting on his heels and skipping stones across the surface of the creek, and wondered if he'd struggled with even half the doubts she still had before coming to his decision. She gave an ironic smile; apart from her late father, Mitch was the most self-assured man God had ever moulded. Men like Mitch didn't have doubts, because they believed in their own infallibility and he'd passed more than a little of his arrogance on to his daughter.

It wouldn't matter how long Vanessa kept arguing her point of view; Angie was too much her father's daughter not to follow her own mind.

'When's the wedding?' she asked with resignation.

No other question could have guaranteed Mitch's complete attention so quickly, she mused, as he spun instantly to face her.

The smile he bestowed upon her appeared tinged with pride and it caused her heart to double-shuffle before resuming a regular, though somewhat faster, beat.

'Four weeks' time,' he said, pushing his hat back on his head. 'That's the minimum waiting time in this state. They're going in to get the licence today.'

'I suppose she wants to have it here?' Vanessa speculated, and a tiny sigh passed her lips at the nod of confirmation. 'That means I'm facing another three cross-country air trips.'

'*Three*?' He frowned. 'How do you figure that?'

'My flight back to Perth the day after tomorrow,' she ticked off the fingers on her left hand. 'The trip back for the wedding and the subsequent return flight.'

'But what about all the preparations that need to be done here? Angie's hoping you'll help her organise everything.'

'Mitch, how much organising is a quiet family wedding going to take? The head-count on our side isn't going to run much beyond twenty,' she told him, refusing to let his amused grin to affect her. 'How many people could Craig possibly want to invite?'

'I'm not sure, but last night Angie's guest numbers were running into three figures. And that was just with what was coming off the top of her head!'

'*What? That's crazy*! The house isn't big enough! And what about caterers?' Honestly, the guy had no idea what was involved!

'Don't worry,' he said. 'My housekeeper and her husband used to run a catering business. And I think Angie will go with my idea of using a marquee rather than—'

'You're out of your mind! You can't pull off what you pair obviously intend will rival anything Buckingham Palace has seen, in *four weeks*! Besides, don't you think that in the circumstances something a little more...more *understated* might be more appropriate?'

Mitch looked aghast at the suggestion.

'I thought you said you didn't want Angie to think we were embarrassed by her—'

'I don't! I'm not! But...'

'But?'

'I can't possibly organise anything on that scale long-distance. It'd mean I'd have to stay here.'

'Ah, you're worried about being too far from your business.'

No! Vanessa wanted to scream. I'm worried about being too close to you! God, how could she cope with the full-scale war which had been raging between her hormones and her common sense for another month!

'Look, you're free to use the phone and fax as much as you like,' he said generously, while wearing a smirk which suggested he found her venture into the world of business amusing. 'After all, as you're half-owner of Brayburn, fifty per cent of all its expenses are deducted from your share of the profits anyway.'

'You're all heart!' she snapped, turning from his self-satisfied expression and marching to the bike. 'Now, would you mind taking me back to the house now so I can begin running up my half of the phone bill?'

A child could have crawled the distance from the creek to the bike *backwards* in the time it took Mitch to cover it. He was plainly in no hurry, and when she thought of how much he expected her to accomplish in four weeks she was spurred to speech.

'C'mon, Mitch! Surely you have some cows or something that are long overdue your complete and utter attention today?'

He looked thoughtful, then grinned. 'Nope.'

'Well, pretend you do! I'm in a hurry.'

'You want to drive?' he asked, the picture of innocence.

'Unfortunately I don't know how to, otherwise only one of us would still be standing here!'

'Hop on—I'll teach you.'

'I don't want to learn!'

'Sure you do,' he counted with a sexy smile. 'You've always loved learning new things.'

Vanessa's stomach dropped and her pulse-rate soared at his very obvious innuendo. She wasn't going to play his game.

'Mitch,' she said through clenched teeth. 'I do not have any desire to learn how to ride a trail-bike. I—'

'OK, so what do you have a desire for right at this minute?' he enquired softly.

Illicit excitement skidded down her spine, paralysing her, so that Mitch had no difficulty in shortening the distance between them to mere centimetres.

'Nothing! I don't desire nothing.'

Nothing? That didn't come out right, she thought. 'Anything!' she shouted, confident she was grammatically correct this time. 'I mean anything!'

A huge smile spread across his face.

'How about,' he suggested, moving his hands to her hips and bringing their bodies into contact. 'Anything and everything?'

One by one Vanessa's internal organs reached meltdown point. When she felt her nipples harden beneath her blouse, she wanted to scream with frustration and self-disgust. Couldn't her body muster even a small token rejection of him? Why couldn't she fight? If she kicked and screamed she'd be safe. Mitch wasn't the type of man to use force. So why wasn't she lashing out at him this very minute?

'You are so very, very beautiful, Nessa. Even more beautiful than you were ten years ago.' He reached out and stroked her hair, then lifted a handful of strands from her shoulders and let them fall back one by one. 'A rainbow of copper and gold,' he whispered, lowering his mouth to hers.

She thought about resisting, she really did, but the moment Mitch's lips met hers the taste of him sent her dizzy. Wonderfully, gloriously dizzy! And suddenly all Vanessa's reasons for resisting were made to seem shallow and stupid. When his tongue probed the centre of her lips, her entire skeletal system collapsed.

Instinctively her hands grasped his shoulders for support and the twitch of male muscle beneath her fingers ricocheted off every nerve-ending in her body and an excited quiver shook her.

Mitch's mouth became more demanding and Vanessa revelled in the sensations he was reawakening in her. The feel of his hands on her body after a decade of abstinence was glorious. Everything about this man was both achingly familiar and temptingly new, and she doubted her craving for him could ever be satisfied in this lifetime. Nothing had changed between them. Nothing...

A biting chill seeped through her body, reminding Vanessa of why the kiss had to end.

Lowering her hands, she pushed hard at his broad chest, catching him off guard, and, once free of his arms, moved so that the bike stood between them.

'Nessa?' He frowned at her with desire heavy eyes.

'Don't call me that. And please...don't touch me again.'

'Come again?'

She shook her head, too emotionally swamped to put her feelings into words.

Mitch took a step towards her, but she moved, keeping the distance between them. 'Ah, honey.'

'It's over between us, Mitch. And I'm not interested in any reminiscing.'

'But why?' He looked stunned. 'You can't pretend the spark that used to exist between us is dead.'

'Oh, Mitch,' she said fervently. 'I'd give almost anything to be able to extinguish that bloody *spark*, as you call it.'

'Then what the hell is your problem? I want you, you want me—nothing's changed.'

'Exactly! Nothing's changed in your eyes and everything has in mine.' She shook her head sadly at the confusion in his face. He really didn't understand.

'Mitch, if I thought I could handle an affair with you I'd probably be in your bed so fast your head would swim. But, despite what you think, *neither* of us is equipped to handle an affair.'

'Well, I mightn't have had the opportunity of doing a detailed inspection of you, lady! But rest assured I'm carrying as much as every other physically healthy male my age!'

'Mitch, that's not—'

'Jeez, Vanessa, eleven years ago you were more than convinced I was capable of carrying on an affair! In fact you were so bloody certain I *was* having one that you threw yourself on to a half-broken horse when you were *seven months pregnant*!'

The pain inflicted by his words was so intense, she was sure her heart had ruptured and was pouring blood into her chest cavity. She sank to her knees.

'Vanessa!'

How strange that the look of anguish on Mitch's face seemed to mirror what she was feeling, she thought. Then, as everything around her began to blur, she squeezed her eyes tight against the tears, blocking him out.

Crying would solve nothing. She wouldn't cry. No matter how much she wanted to, she wouldn't. *She would not cry.* But oh, how she wanted to!

She wanted to cry about so many things. Things that she'd had and lost, and things she'd wanted and never had. She wanted to cry and cry until her head ached from crying, and she wanted to keep crying until exhaustion and sleep claimed her and then... And then she wanted to wake up and discover that everything, *every rotten thing* that had ever happened in her life had been nothing more than a bad dream.

Yet Vanessa knew from past experience that tears and wishful thinking were both unproductive and unrealistic, so she forced herself to face the facts instead. She'd always known that Mitch held her responsible for the loss of his son. Hell! Even after all the counselling she'd had, in the far recess of her mind *she* still held herself responsible. Mitch's finally verbalising his feelings, didn't alter anything. Nothing could.

What had happened had happened. The past was out of her hands and all she held now was the present. She had to stay focused on that. She had to!

'Dear God, Vanessa, I didn't mean to—'

Shrugging free of the hand resting on her shoulder, she got to her feet.

'Don't apologise, Mitch,' she said, pushing her hair from her face. 'You've kept a lid on it for eleven years. I couldn't have if our situations were reversed.'

She shook her head when he opened his mouth to speak. 'No, don't say anything more. Just take me back to the house.'

CHAPTER FOUR

ONCE back at the house, Vanessa wanted nothing more than to lock herself in her bedroom.

She needed time to analyse the whirlpool of emotions raging within her...too many of which were linked to Mitch. But the presence of her daughter, and the need to resolve their differences, meant a mother-daughter heart-to-heart had to be her first priority.

That discussion lasted the remainder of the morning, ending only when Craig came to pick up Angela so they could go and apply for their marriage licence.

'Mum, here's a list of things that simply *must* be organised today!'

Vanessa had hoped her daughter's absence would give her a few hours' respite from having to deal with the damn wedding!

'Can't these wait, Angela? Surely one day won't make any difference?'

'Mum!' The tone was a mix of horror and betrayal. 'You promised you'd help! That you'd support me now.'

One glance at the trembling bottom lip of her daughter had Vanessa vowing to carry out the task. Consequently after lunch, she began chasing up quotes for the hire of chairs, tables and marquees, before contacting the local priest about performing the ceremony.

The hour-long conversation with Father Fitzgerald was an ordeal despite the old Irishman's jovial chit chat.

It had been Father Fitzgerald who'd married herself and

Mitch, declaring that although they'd been overly eager in consummating their relationship he had no doubts that their love would endure the everyday trials which plagued most marriages. Though on the day she'd made her vows she hadn't anticipated most of those everyday trials being the deliberate work of her own father. Nor had she ever envisaged Mitch's feelings for Brayburn would become so obsessive that he barely had time for a wife.

So during the entire conversation Vanessa had been waiting for him to make some sanctimonious remark about how she'd violated the bonds of holy matrimony in getting divorced. No such accusation had been forthcoming, but nevertheless by the time she hung up the phone she was feeling mentally and emotionally drained. The timing of Mitch's housekeeper couldn't have been better.

'Cup of tea, Ms Brayburn?'

'Tea sounds divine.' She smiled at the older woman. 'Why don't you join me?'

Cora literally beamed at the invitation and quickly returned with a second cup.

'Have you worked for Mitch long?' Vanessa asked, pouring the tea from a teapot that until today she'd only ever seen in the china cabinet. Cora reached out and touched her cheek and reflexively she looked at the older woman's face.

'You must look at me when you speak,' the woman instructed.

Vanessa frowned.

'I'm deaf. I need to see your mouth.'

'Oh, I'm sorry. Of course, lip-reading.' Vanessa smiled feebly. 'I...no one told me.'

'It's flattering that Mitch and Angie can forget it's necessary.' The woman smiled. 'I'm real good as long as the person speaking is looking at me.'

'I'll try and remember, but I'm sure I'll slip up,' Vanessa replied.

'Everyone does at first.'

'And please, call me Vanessa.'

The woman repeated the name perfectly, smiling when Vanessa nodded her approval.

'Now what was it you said before?'

'I asked how long you'd worked for Mitch.'

'Three years next January. I like it here. He's a good man, your husband.'

'*Ex*-husband,' Vanessa corrected. 'And although I could question the compliment on personal grounds, I do know he's always been considered a fair man to work for.'

Cora chuckled. 'I think you want to change the subject, Vanessa.'

She simply smiled and helped herself to a freshly baked biscuit.

'Mmm. These are great. Cora, there's something I'd like to ask you. But please, if it's an imposition, I want you to say so.'

'I'm nothing if not frank, Vanessa.' She chuckled and added drily, 'Ask the boss.'

Vanessa wasn't particularly keen to see Mitch again any time soon, much less speak with him, but it was obvious the housekeeper thought him only one stage from God.

'Cora, it wouldn't take a genius to work out I'm not thrilled about my daughter's marriage. But I am her mother and despite the fact that nothing would make me happier than to have her change her mind, I'm anxious this wedding turn out to be everything she wants it to be.' Recalling the indecently large crowd her daughter wanted to invite, she added, 'Within the bounds of good taste! If I get my way!'

Cora laughed. 'I spoke to Angela this morning. Quantity not quality was foremost in her mind.'

'Exactly. But given that I can convince her to reduce the numbers, would you be interested in supervising the caterers?

I realise four weeks isn't very much time, but Mitch mentioned you and your late husband ran a catering firm.'

'Did he also tell you it went bust?'

'No. I'm sorry. I...'

'That's all right, pet. It was Stan's gambling that was the problem, not the standard of the cooking.' Cora laughed and Vanessa knew it was a response to the relieved expression she was wearing. 'I'll be pleased to organise the catering.'

'Thank you,' Vanessa said. 'That's one thing I can tick off as done.'

Vanessa spent the remainder of the afternoon trying to juggle her business calendar so that her absence from Perth during the next four weeks caused the minimum disruption. Although she had the utmost confidence in her store manager and two regular sales clerks, she hated not being available to supervise the store's first summer parade of the season. Yet even though she had grave doubts about her daughter's decision to marry, she would never have placed her business commitments over Angie.

An hour before dinner, she took herself off to the family-room to pursue the list of plans her daughter had thrust at her during the afternoon. It was blatantly obvious that Angela intended ignoring her mother's lack of enthusiasm for the upcoming nuptials.

'What's that?'

Her heart-rate doubled at the unexpected sound of Mitch's voice, but she managed to keep the tone of her response even.

'Our daughter's wedding plans.'

'Oh. So where is she?'

'Probably where she's been since she got home,' Vanessa replied. 'On the phone.'

'She's been on the phone for *two hours*? Doing what?'

'Announcing her upcoming nuptials.'

Mitch grinned. 'I guess the phone bill might be up a bit this quarter.'

'The phone bill will be the least of your worries.'

'Uh?'

She picked up the A4 notepad beside her and gave it to him.

'What's this?' he asked frowning.

'The first draft of your daughter's guest list and her planned menu.'

'*All* these people?'

'Plus some additional relatives of Craig's. She said she'd have the final number tomorrow.'

A panicked look claimed his face. 'Good God! There aren't this many names in the Bible! What's A.F. after them mean?'

'And friend,' she said coolly, peeping over the top of the magazine she held in front of her face. He looked almost catatonic with dread.

'All these pages are wedding details?'

'Mmm. Although she hasn't settled on a colour scheme yet, but the menu is definite.'

She watched Mitch frantically leaf through another half-dozen pages until he found it. His face, as he read, grew paler and paler.

'She wants *yearling veal* as the main course?'

'I think her choice is good.'

'Sure! If you want to wipe out our entire herd in one go!'

'Now, Mitch. You're exaggerating,' she said, fighting to keep laughter at bay for a while longer. 'You'll still have a few calves left.'

'Not funny, Vanessa…'

It was from where she was sitting!

'You'll have to talk to her. Tell her this is beyond reasonable.'

'Why me?'

'Well…because you're her mother,' he said as if she shouldn't have to ask.

'Yes, but you're her father.'

'I *know* that! But mothers are supposed to organise all the…
the…formal stuff. Fathers just have to pay the bill.'

'Then where's the problem?' asked innocently. 'I said I'd
help organise it and I will. It won't be easy getting everything
together for so a large number, in such a short time, but I dare
say I'll manage.'

'Damn it, Vanessa! Can't you get your head out of that
book! I'm trying to talk to you.'

She bit the inside of her mouth. 'I know, I can hear you,
but I'm trying to decide what dinner set we'll have. Angie
wants something—'

'Let me guess,' Mitch barked. 'Expensive?'

'Elegant,' she said holding the magazine higher. 'And I
agree.'

'This morning you wanted ''understated''.'

'This morning you didn't.'

'Yes, but I never envisaged… This'll cost thousands!'

'Tens of thousands, I should think.'

At Mitch's gasp she sneaked a look. He looked as if he'd
been poleaxed, but she couldn't resist adding, 'Of course, then
there's the dress…'

'Vanessa, have you lost your mind?'

'She's your only daughter…'

'Thank God for that!'

Even though she bit the inside of her mouth she couldn't
stop the giggle which bubbled from her throat. Instantly the
magazine was snatched from her grasp and Mitch's thunderous
face loomed over her.

'Why, you…you…'

She collapsed against the back of the lounge as silent laughter shook her body.

'I just couldn't resist…' she stammered. 'Oh, Mitch, you
should have seen your face. Heard…the *panic* in…your
voice.'

'You never had any intention of approving this, did you?'

She shook her head. 'Not in a million years.'

'I'd wring your pretty neck—' amusement now lit his handsome features '—if it didn't mean I'd get stuck organising this...circus on my own.'

'I'm sure you'd do wonderfully. Would you like to reconsider the hasty reprieve?'

'Uh-uh.' He bestowed a heart-stopping smile on her. 'You aren't getting out of it that easily.'

With the sensuality of his earlier smile still attacking her body, Vanessa simply prayed she'd get out of it without suffering any more damage to her heart!

'I'm having a drink; you want one?'

'Eh? No, I don't think so. I...'

'It'll give us a chance to prune that guest-list back a bit. Angie intends sending out the invitations tomorrow,' he said.

Vanessa was uneasy. Even doing something as innocuous as culling the guest-list with Mitch was fraught with danger. For as long as she could remember he'd been able to prod her anger or stroke her passion as no one else could. They'd never been able to walk the safe middle ground of friendship, so it was stupid to think they could start now. Yet what choice did she have?

She was obliged to organise the wedding and any reluctance on her part to co-operate with him or Angela would be perceived as, at best, delaying tactics and at worst a deliberate attempt to sabotage the event. Angela had already accused her of *that* when Vanessa had pointed out that, even with her fashion connections, finding a dress such as Angie wanted in four weeks was going to be nigh on impossible.

If she hoped to convince the girl her guest list was too big, it would help to have Mitch back her on the subject.

'OK, I'll have a Scotch and dry. No—'

'I remember,' he interrupted. 'No ice.'

She nodded, looking away from his charming half-smile. If she was going to have any hope of getting through the next hour or so she was going to have to ensure things remained on a businesslike level. She picked up the notepad and a pen.

'Right, then,' she said in the tone she reserved for dealing with pushy sales reps. 'As far as I'm concerned we should keep the numbers to one hundred. Max.'

'Sounds reasonable,' Mitch said putting her drink on the coffee-table in front, before settling himself into the corner of the sofa.

Her body felt the effect of his solid frame on the overstuffed lounge through her buttocks and she shifted further away, masking her intent to put extra distance between them by turning towards him. She didn't look at him—she just turned towards him.

'So who do *you* want to ask?' she queried, taking a sip of her drink and sparing him only the shortest of glances over the top of the glass.

'Haven't really thought about it.' He frowned. 'Cam, I guess, and—'

The mention of his younger brother brought a smile to Vanessa. 'I wonder if he's still seeing the blonde he had with him when he came to Perth last time?'

'You saw him when he was in Perth?' Mitch was instantly alert.

'He always calls me when he comes over for any of the big racing carnivals. Why shouldn't he?' She knew she sounded defensive, but damn it, just because she and Mitch were divorced, there was no reason she couldn't keep in contact with other members of his family.

'No reason. He never mentioned it, that's all.' He watched his glass as if fascinated by the ice floating in the amber liquid. 'The way you left here gave everyone the impression you wanted to cut all ties with your old life.'

Vanessa could hear the underlying irritation in his voice.

She shrugged. 'Cam never presumed to judge me or my actions, unlike most of the people around here.' The few people she'd spoken to from the region had made it abundantly clear that no matter what the provocation, a wife didn't leave her husband. Her brother-in-law Cameron, a racehorse breeder from Scone, had been the only person to continue to offer her his friendship.

'People round here aren't like that.'

'Not usually, perhaps,' she conceded. 'But where you're concerned they are. They have Mitch Randall on such a bloody pedestal that you could probably run a child pornography ring and they'd find a way of justifying it!'

'That's rubbish and you know it!' he snapped. 'But considering the way you just upped and vanished with my daughter, what did you expect?'

Vanessa gave an ironic smile. 'Exactly what I got. After all you were the poor, noble jackaroo, who'd not only done the right thing by marrying Jack Brayburn's spoilt, promiscuous daughter, but also managed to transform Brayburn from being simply a "valuable and historic property" into a money-making one as well.' She shook her head slowly. 'In their eyes you were perfect and I was a spoilt ungrateful bitch who took after her mother.'

'I wouldn't have expected such bitterness from you, Vanessa.'

'I'm not bitter,' she said. 'At least not any more.'

'But you admit you were.'

'It's not as if I didn't have reason to be.' She stared at him. 'It's not as if *all* the facts were ever made public knowledge.'

'Meaning Rachel.'

Bile welled up in Vanessa so quickly that she thought she was going to throw up. If Mitch had hit her it wouldn't have hurt as much as hearing him bring up the name of the woman who'd been the catalyst in the events leading up to the loss of her baby. For the second time in one day he was deliberately reminding her of the one thing she wanted to avoid.

'Mitch, if you mention that woman's name again I'm heading straight back to Perth. You got that?'

'Vanessa, I *swear* I never had an affair with her!'

'I don't want to discuss any of this! Do you hear me? None of it!'

'Every person from here to hell can hear you!' he grabbed her shoulders and forced her to look at him. 'Vanessa, we *have* to talk about this. We have to talk about what happened...what happened to us, what happened to Samuel.'

'No! It's over. It's finished.' God, why was he doing this to her? 'I'm done talking about it.'

'Damn it, Vanessa! We've *never* talked about it,' he released her to run a weary hand through his hair. 'Please, Vanessa. I need you to understand exactly what happened between Rachel and me. *I* need to talk about it.'

'What's to talk about?'

'Oh, c'mon—'

'No, I mean it! What the hell is there to talk about after all these years? I thought you were having an affair. You deny the affair although you admitted you did consider having one. Then I find you in the arms of...' She gave a bitter laugh. 'Let's say "the other woman"—clichéd, of course, but it works for me! And *silly me* is so shocked, I jump on a half-broken horse and end up getting thrown.'

'You should have trusted me! At the very least—'

'Trusted you! You'd already admitted you found Rachel attractive!'

'The fact that I'd told you should have been—'

'Should have been what? *I found you in one another's arms!*'

'It wasn't the way it looked! You judged me on circumstantial evidence!'

'Oh, well, sorr-y! My fault! I should have recognised the difference between mental infidelity and physical infidelity! Forgive me, I was the one in the wrong! It's my fault, OK?

That make you happy? I take full responsibility for everything that happened! I was—'

'Vanessa, you're making yourself hysterical.'

'Hysterical! Hah! You think this is hysteria? No, Mitch, if you wanted to see hysteria, you should have been at Perth airport a week after I left you! Compared to that this is sedate!'

She couldn't help the bitter laugh that escaped, but she was past worrying about keeping her own counsel.

'You want to know what happened? I sat down in the gutter outside the terminal, in freezing cold rain, hugging a suitcase under one arm and Angie under the other, and I cried. At first I cried because I didn't know what to do. But after a while I was crying because I didn't know how to stop! I didn't even know why I was crying.' She hugged her arms around herself as the remembered incident caused her to shudder. Yet she knew that if she stopped now she'd spare herself nothing.

'I cried and cried and cried. I cried until a nineteen-year-old social work student came along and decided I was her chance at some hands-on experience.' She paused and turned to Mitch.

'You want to know why I didn't contact you for three months? It's because I was in such an emotional state that I could barely distinguish one day from the next! Hysterical, Mitch? This doesn't even come close! But believe me, I'm way past caring whether you *had* Rachel mentally, physically or telepathically! Have you got that? *I don't care.* Now if you have a problem with your conscience unburden yourself on someone else!'

She started towards the door, but he blocked her path.

'Vanessa, I...'

Though trembling from head to foot, she tried to look lethal as she turned to him. 'Yes?'

'I don't know... We *have* to talk.'

'No, we don't. Just because you want a blow-by-blow description, it doesn't mean I have to give you one. The subject is closed.'

'Dammit, Vanessa! I deserve—'

'Don't start telling me what *you* deserve, Mitch! Because I'm not interested!'

She pulled open the door and stepped into the hall with Mitch right on her heels, but the sight of Angie and Craig walking arm-in-arm towards them stopped them dead.

'Oh, great, you're both here!' Angie said. 'You can tell us what you've decided about the wedding!'

Vanessa groaned. She did not need this! She really didn't!

'Well, we...er...haven't really discussed it yet—' she hedged.

'You mean you and Daddy haven't talked it over?'

'No,' Mitch answered. 'But a lot was said, wasn't it, Vanessa?' His eyes were cutting, his tone so 'pleasant', only she knew he wasn't referring to the pending wedding.

'Then let's do it now!' Angie said cheerfully, already dragging Craig back into the room Vanessa and Mitch had just left.

'Er...no,' Vanessa started.

'Why not?'

'Yes, Vanessa, *why not?*' Mitch parroted his daughter. 'Let's get the bloody thing over and done with!'

Reluctant to cause a scene, she returned to the room. Vanessa knew she'd have a fight on her hands just keeping a check on the emotion pouring through her, but she was very aware of the need to keep her personal feelings about the past separate from the present. For Angela's sake.

With Craig and Angie sitting on the sofa, Vanessa chose one of the armchairs, but when Mitch moved to the other directly opposite her she lowered her eyes to the notepad she held to avoid meeting his gaze.

'Right, for starters,' Mitch wasted no time jumping into the subject, 'the guest list is restricted to one hundred!'

'What?' Angela wailed. 'No! We can't possibly cut the numbers back to one hundred and invite everyone I want to,' she protested.

'Then you won't be able to ask everyone you want to, will you?'

'But that's not fair!' Angie looked heartbroken.

Vanessa was furious! Damned right it wasn't fair! Mitch had no right taking his anger at *her* out on Angela! She sent him a telling look that threatened murder if he came out with one more sarcastic or obnoxious comment.

Mitch met her gaze for several moments before running a frustrated hand through his hair. He turned to his daughter.

'I'm sorry, honey. I'm in a lousy mood. Forgive me?'

Angie produced one of those instant mood changes only expectant mothers could manage.

'Sure, Daddy.'

Mitch sent Vanessa a smug grin and, not trusting that a snide remark wouldn't follow, she quickly turned to her daughter.

'Angela, I really do think your father's right—'

'But of course only in this particular instance,' Mitch said. 'Your mother's faith in me is strictly selective.'

Vanessa felt the colour rise in her face as both youngsters looked askance at her.

'Most men are hopeless with wedding details!' she laughed, hoping the two youngsters would think she and Mitch were only kidding about. The weak smiles they offered weren't exactly convincing.

'Now, Angie,' she started, aware of Mitch watching her intently. 'I know you had about two hundred and twenty people you felt you *had* to invite, but I—'

'A reception that size is way too expensive,' Mitch stated.

'Daddy, this *is* my wedding.'

'We know that, Angie,' Vanessa said quickly. 'But, well— I feel anything over one-fifty is really *tacky*.'

'Not to mention expensive,' Mitch insisted.

'You really think that many would be tacky?' Angie asked, typically ignoring the financial aspect of things.

'Yes I do. I think one hundred would be the ideal number.'

'Not to mention cheaper,' Mitch said. Vanessa sent him a 'let me handle this' look, which he ignored, tacking on, 'Much cheaper.'

'Oh, Dad, you aren't going to be a cheapskate about this, are you? I can't believe you'd think of money at—'

'Cheapskate! No! Of course not! I...I'm not worried about the money, it's just that...'

Vanessa shook her head, wondering how much further he could put his foot into his mouth.

'...I don't want things to look *tacky*.'

'OK, that sounds good. One hundred people and hang the expense!' Angela clapped her hands.

Mitch blinked as if he'd missed something along the way. Then as the implications of what he'd said dawned he slumped back in his chair and looked heavenwards. Hah! Vanessa thought maliciously, maybe now he'd shut up and let her handle this!

'Right, now as far as I'm concerned, I only have five people I'd like to ask,' Vanessa said. 'My friend Susan Cleary and her daughter Kassie—'

'No prob, Mum!' Angie interrupted. 'I've decided I'm going to ask Kassie to be flower girl.'

'Great! Well, the only other people I want to invite are the Millers and Reece Drummond.'

'Who's Reece Drummond?' Mitch asked.

'A designer friend of mine.'

'He's gay, uh?'

'No, Mitch, he's not gay. Just because a guy has a flair for designing women's clothes, it doesn't mean he's gay.'

'Right,' Mitch said, implying just the opposite.

Vanessa gave her attention back to the list.

'Now you've got your uncle Cam down here, but you better add "and friend". The day Cameron Randall goes *anywhere* stag will be the day they carry him out in a pine box!'

The remark brought an amused chuckle from Angie, who turned to Craig and quickly began a run-down of a few of the more bizarre women who had graced the arm of Cameron Randall over the years.

'There was even one,' she said, 'who used to come up here all the time even after Cam had dumped her!'

Vanessa felt her veins ice over and goose-bumps rise on her skin.

'Her name was Rach—'

'That's enough, Angie!' Mitch's voice boomed the interruption and caused both youngsters to start. 'Forget the side-tracking and let's get on with things,' he added. 'I can't spend all night doing this!'

Whatever else Mitch had pressing to do that night, it wasn't work, Vanessa decided a few hours later when she went to his study.

He was sitting in front of a blank computer screen, slumped low in the leather chair with his booted feet propped on the desk and his hands linked behind his head.

For several minutes she allowed herself the luxury of watching him.

No matter how much or how often she wished otherwise, no man would ever be able to touch her on such an elemental level as Mitch did. What she'd felt with him went way beyond what she'd once tried to convince herself was only an overwhelming lust. No, it was more than lust. But it wasn't anything as honest as love either, she acknowledged sadly.

Whatever the force was that had bound them so fiercely to each other as kids, it hadn't been strong enough to hold them together in adulthood. The question was, would there ever come a time when she could be around Mitch and not feel it lurking?

'You coming in or are you just going to stand there all night?'

His words didn't surprise her; she'd known he was aware of her presence. She walked over and propped herself on the edge of the desk, tipping her head forward a little so that her hair curtained her face from his view.

'Firstly I want to thank you, for cutting off Angie's...*little story* earlier.' She smiled in an effort to dispel her own discomfort. 'I appreciate it.'

Mitch shrugged. 'Believe me, if *she'd* seen the look on your face at the time she'd have stopped of her own accord.' He pushed her hair aside and looked into her eyes. 'You really do believe the worst, don't you?'

The soft disappointment behind the words and his nearness raised momentary doubts in her, but the image of what she'd witnessed all those years ago flashed into her mind and quelled them.

'I know what I saw, Mitch,' she said firmly and moved from the desk to put some distance between them. Within visual range Mitch was a distraction; within touchable range he was temptation personified.

'Look,' she said from the safety of the bookcase on the far wall, 'I didn't come in here to rehash our earlier argument.'

'Oh, you mean you want to pick a fight on an entirely different subject?' His teasing grin annoyed simply because she found herself struggling to hold back a smile.

'No! I don't want any more fighting between us.'

'Now this sounds *very* promising. I'm a strong believer in the kiss-and-make-up theory.'

Vanessa's body temperature jumped several degrees, but even as she tried to credit the cause to anger she couldn't stop herself from admiring Mitch's sexy, laughing eyes.

'I'm not,' she said. Then, because her voice didn't sound a

bit convincing, added, 'In our case, Mitch, it would be like putting a Band-aid on a corpse.'

Leaden silence and eye-to-eye combat followed her words. For several seconds a million different emotions and accusations seemed to ricochet between the two of them, then, fearing she might unwittingly reveal or perhaps see more than she wanted to, Vanessa lowered her lashes.

'OK, Vanessa,' Mitch said as if he was bored with events. 'What's the punchline? Why are you here?'

'For Angie's sake I want your agreement that you'll stop dragging the past up every second minute.'

'Forget it!'

She stared at him not believing his response. He was supposed to be agreeably adult about this, the way he'd been when she'd mentally rehearsed this scene in her bedroom.

'Why?' she asked.

'Because, sweetheart,' he sneered, 'you owe me an explanation—'

'*I* owe *you* an explanation?'

'OK, then you owe me the *right* of explanation,' he amended. 'Even homicidal maniacs get an opportunity to defend themselves.'

'Mitch, if you want absolution have Father Fitzgerald hear your confession,' she said. 'Because I've spent ten years putting the past behind me; I've dealt with it once I'm not prepared to do it again. Not for you, not even for Angela.'

Mitch shook his head. 'If that were true, Nessa, you wouldn't be afraid to discuss things. You haven't dealt with the past, you've blocked it out.'

'Believe what you wish, Mitch—'

'Just as you do, huh?' he asked bitterly. 'Disregard the facts and simply believe what it suits you to!'

Vanessa closed her eyes in an effort to distance herself from the accusation which pinched at both her heart and her conscience. Perhaps he was right, she conceded silently. Had the need for emotional survival distorted her thinking? To contemplate such things now, though, would undo what little control she still had. She'd do it later. Later when she was alone.

She opened her eyes and looked at Mitch. 'If I thought for one second talking about the past would change it—' she blinked back tears '—believe me, God Himself wouldn't be able to shut me up.'

The pain in Mitch's face once again mirrored her own and she had to look away. After a moment her eyes again sought Mitch. He was standing beside the French doors and staring out into the darkness, the desk lamp projecting his image onto the glass somehow made him look fragile. Vanessa frowned. 'Fragile' wasn't a word synonymous with Mitch Randall, and his next words proved it.

'I have no intention of letting you pretend we don't have a past, Vanessa. If you want to adopt a selective memory fine, but I don't believe in self-delusion. However,' he said, 'I will try to keep our personal problems away from Angela and Craig until the wedding.'

'Thank you for that much, at least.'

'Considering how grudgingly you give your thanks, I was a real fool to ever think I had your trust!' He gave a bitter laugh. 'Tell me, Nessa how does someone go about winning your trust?'

'Trust isn't something you win, Mitch, it's something you earn.'

He smiled, licked one finger and chalked up a point to her on an invisible scoreboard.

She stared at him, wondering how even now just the sight of him could make her heart beat faster. Why was it no other man ever had? Desperate to escape the suffocating emotions and memories crowding the room, she started for the door.

'Er—one more thing, Vanessa.'

'What now?' she asked tersely.

'This Reece Drummond you want to invite to the wedding...'

'What about him?'

'What is he?'

She gave him a blank look. 'He's a fashion designer.'

'I know that already!' Mitch folded his arms aggressively. 'I mean what's he to you? Are you lovers?'

'No!' At his satisfied smirk Vanessa wanted to bite off her tongue. 'Not that it's any of your business!'

'The hell it's not! You're my—'

'I'm not *your* anything!' The look on his face as she said the words suddenly made his questions crystal-clear. 'Good God, you're jealous!'

'Don't sound so amazed,' he said, then ran his eyes over her body in a slowly suggestive way that almost burned her. 'Since I had you first, the idea of not being able to have you now hardly makes me feel magnanimous towards those who might. Do you have a current lover?'

Vanessa wanted to slap him into the middle of next week! 'Why you...you...'

'Just for the record,' he said conversationally. 'Did Cam ever put the hard word on you?'

Her gasp was audible, but her lungs didn't feel as if they'd actually sucked in any air. She was furious! So livid she could barely speak.

'How...how dare you? I... We...' She swore and stamped her foot, the sudden action seemingly jolting her words into coherency. 'Cameron and I are friends! Nothing more! I can't believe you could even think such a thing, much less voice it!'

Mitch was laughing as if her outrage was totally unfounded. 'Well, Cam did have quite a crush on you, when he was thirteen.'

'Yeah and I was eighteen, married to his brother and the

mother of his niece!' Vanessa roared. 'Not to mention the fact that the infatuation died about two weeks later!'

'True,' Mitch nodded. 'But now five years isn't such a difference, and once you divorced me...' Mitch gave her a speculative glance.

'Oh, for God's sake, Mitch—' she threw her arms in the air '—are you on drugs?'

Mitch burst out laughing. It was then Vanessa realised that he'd been deliberately provoking her.

'You know I've got a good mind to go to Cam and tell him what you've just said!' She glared at him. 'The trouble is, he'd probably die laughing before I could convince him to punch your teeth in for me!'

Mitch sobered and looked at her. His smile was gentle. 'I'm not so sure he would—die laughing, that is. I've no doubt he'd cheerfully punch my teeth in, and what's more...' He sighed. 'I'd deserve it. I'm sorry, Vanessa.'

'So you should be.'

'You know, for a time there I really was jealous of my kid brother and the relationship you and he used to share whenever he came to stay.'

Vanessa blinked in disbelief. 'But that...that was stupid.'

'Yeah, right, just because any time he was here you'd spend hour upon hour with one another.'

'Mitch, we were *friends*. Nothing more. He was interested in how my correspondence studies were going and we used talk about them!'

'You never bothered to talk to *me* about them, though, did you? But then, you didn't think I was smart enough.'

'That's not fair! I never thought any such thing! And besides, what use would trying to talk to you about studying for my matriculation have done? *You* never wanted me to do it!'

'Right! Because I couldn't see the point!'

'The point was, I needed to do *something* with myself once

Angela started school! I was sick of washing clothes and scrubbing toilets—'

'I hired a housekeeper so you wouldn't have to!'

'That's right you did! And that left me with absolutely nothing to do! I was paralysed with boredom. My brain was vegetating!'

For an instant Mitch looked as if she'd punched him in the stomach. Then his features turned from pained shock to an ironic sneer.

'Which is exactly what your old man predicted would happen if you married me.'

Under his embittered gaze Vanessa was forced to look away. There was no doubt her late father could take a lot of credit for undermining the stability of their marriage while he was alive. Prior to the wedding he'd pretended to be supportive of the union, but afterwards his niggling assaults on Mitch had been regularly and publicly voiced.

When Vanessa had asked him why he'd been so supportive of the marriage when she and Mitch had first gone to him, he'd laughingly told her that he'd have married her off to Hitler if it meant defeating his ex-wife's plans.

She physically shuddered, at how her own father had coldbloodedly used her as a weapon against the woman who'd left him.

She looked at the handsome but hard planes of Mitch's face. As much as he'd disliked her father, the two men shared many terrifyingly similar traits. The stubborn determination not to be bested was one, and the obsessive need to make Brayburn the top beef cattle property in the state was another. They'd hated each other's guts on a personal level, but on a professional level Mitch had so admired her father that he'd nearly turned himself inside out trying to emulate him.

'Your old man sure did do a number on us, didn't he?' Mitch said softly.

'Blaming him for all our problems is the soft option, Mitch. He died four years before I left here.'

'I'm not saying he was the *only* problem. But he was the prime one.'

'Maybe.'

'That sounds as if you have other ideas.'

She was tempted to let the comment pass, but it was about time Mitch Randall heard a few home truths!

'OK, maybe Dad was part of the problem, but it was your choice to live here, not mine! I would have been quite happy moving north so you could work the big stations in the gulf country, as you wanted, but you said no!'

'Of course I said no. You were pregnant.'

'Well, I'm sure there have been pregnant women up there before. I didn't want to be responsible for your sacrificing your ambitions.'

'And just how the hell was I suppose to support you and a baby on a nineteen-year-old itinerant jackaroo's wage, huh? At least your father's offer of permanent employment gave me the opportunity of providing you and Angela with a decent home. Call me conservative, but I didn't relish my family living like a bunch of nomads.'

'I still don't understand why you had to sign that contract agreeing to work for him. Or why you never told me about it,' she added accusingly.

'I didn't think it concerned you,' he said flatly.

'My father asks the man I'm going to marry to sign away his soul, and you don't think it's anything to do with me?'

'That's right, it was a business agreement.'

'It was *blackmail*! Dad wanted to make sure I stayed here and he figured that was the surest way of doing it!'

'Your father put *all* his permanent stockmen on contract!' Mitch reminded her. 'Besides, you adored your old man.'

'I didn't know what he was capable of back then,' she said weakly.

'Well, if you didn't, what hope did I have?'

'You still should have told me about the contract before you signed it.'

Mitch ran an aggrieved hand through his hair in a sign of frustration Vanessa knew well.

'I don't want the same thing happening to Angela and Craig,' she stated, and Mitch snapped his glance to meet hers.

'God, you really know how to land an insult, don't you?' he accused. 'You really think I'd pull the same stunt on Angela?'

The pain in his eyes sent guilt flooding through her. She shook her head. No, if nothing else she knew Mitch would never do that.

'I'm sorry. That was unfair,' she said. 'It's just that too much of the past is encroaching on the present and I'm having a hard time keeping the two apart.'

Mitch ran his eyes over the length of her and let out a soft sigh.

'Yeah, me too.' He caught her hand and softly stroked the inside of her wrist. 'Trouble is,' he said huskily, 'it's the good stuff that's knocking *me* to hell.'

'Yes, well, I—' She paused for much needed oxygen. 'I...I...' Trying desperately to ignore the flutter in the pit of her belly, she endeavoured to tug her hand away, but to no avail.

'You what?' Mitch whispered, now moving his free hand to cup her neck.

'I—' She couldn't think of anything but the heat of his touch searing through her body and the burning desire in his blue eyes. Her hormones went wild with memories of their youth and in instant response her pulse jumped into a flamenco tempo. Mitch focused his gaze to her mouth and began lowering his head causing her knees to buckle. Her hands went to his chest, but the feel of his thumping heart beneath them defeated her brain's plan to push him away.

'Oh, Mitch…no.'

'Oh, Nessa, yes,' he smiled. 'Most definitely yes.'

CHAPTER FIVE

PERHAPS if his kiss had been a hard, ruthless assault she might have had a chance, but his teasing gentleness overrode any thought of resistance.

Over and over he brushed his mouth across her bottom lip. So insidiously slowly, and so softly, that at times she felt nothing but the warmth of his breath and the rhythmic slipping of his hands up and down her arm.

A remnant of her reason was urging her to push away from this threat to her sanity, but it was being drowned out by the noise of her blood pumping at top speed and the screams of her overwrought hormones. They weren't satisfied with this half-hearted nibbling! Not when white-hot memories of what his mouth was capable of were fogging up her brain!

She raised her arms to his head to bring it closer, but he resisted and continued his torturously tentative kisses. Frustration and the greed to taste more of him made her impatient.

'Mitch, if you're going to do it, at least do it properly!'

Her body absorbed his soundless chuckle as he hauled her against him and began dragging his hands from her shoulderblades down her spine and over her buttocks. She angled her mouth more aggressively over his, beckoning his tongue into it. It needed little encouragement.

'Better?' he murmured considerably later.

Her response was a heartfelt groan of approval.

As the tide of their passion continued to rise, Vanessa was happy being swept up in it. Wave after wave of sensation crashed over her until she was drenched with emotions only Mitch had ever been able to stir.

She was vaguely aware of him carrying her to the chesterfield. But soon surroundings and time faded in the hot brilliance of his touch and the erotic feeling that lying beneath his body elicited.

Slick, feverish kisses kept pace with two pairs of hands hungry to reacquaint themselves with flesh they'd once known better than their own. While Mitch was struggling with the intricate buttons of her blouse, Vanessa released all the press studs on the front of his shirt with one aggressive tug.

The sight of the tanned expanse of chest made her breath catch. She was mesmerised by the absolute perfection of the man holding her. Totally awed, she trailed the nails of both hands through the soft mesh of hair.

'Ahh…Nessa!'

It might have been the sound of his voice or perhaps the impact of the sensual shudder which rocked his body, but mercifully something jolted her from her dreamlike trance long enough for her to recognise the insanity of what she was doing.

'Oh, dear heaven!'

Her words were panted and might have been misconstrued had she not shoved frantically and forcefully against the chest of the man lying on top of her. His eyes opened in puzzled confusion. A second shove in unison with a lurch of her body sent him rolling on to the floor.

'What the he—'

His voice was thick with arousal and groggy with confusion, his face and eyes disbelieving. Vanessa knew women were called teasers for a lot less, but right now emotional survival was more important to her than fair play. She backed away until almost the width of the room was between them.

'OK,' he said getting to his feet. 'Let me guess, you changed your mind?'

She shook her head. 'I came to my senses.' She paused in the action of buttoning her blouse when the sound of movement indicated his approach. Automatically her hands went up to ward him off.

'Please, Mitch...'

'I always please,' he smirked. 'You know that better than—'

'Stop!' she ordered. When it was obvious he didn't think she meant it, she moved so the armchair was between them.

'Mitch, I'm sorry. I...I didn't mean for that to happen. Let's just forget the whole—'

'The hell I will! What makes you think you can come waltzing back into my life and jerk me around with your passion on, passion off routine!'

'I didn't come waltzing back into your life willingly, Mitch!' He flinched as if she'd slapped him. 'I'm here because of Angela. Nothing else comes into it.'

'What about what's between us, Vanessa?' His voice was suddenly soft. Seductively soft, but she was determined to resist its charm.

'There's nothing between us any more, Mitch. It's over. It's been over for more than ten years.'

'Crap! We practically go up in flames the minute we're in the same room. As we always did.' He shook his head as if despairing of her stubbornness, then produced one of his ironic half-smiles. 'You're every bit as hot for me as I am for you, only you won't admit it. But your body language is almost deafening.' He glanced deliberately at the outline of her aroused breasts.

Vanessa felt a guilty blush rise directly from her loins and flood her face.

'I rest my case,' he said.

'Mitch, we've always had good sex. But that's not enough for me any more.'

'*Good* sex?' he laughed. 'Honey, together we're way past *good*. In fact sex doesn't get any better!'

'No, but love does. At least I think it does.' She added the qualification, because all she had to go on was a gut instinct.

'What's that supposed to mean?'

'Answer me this. Would you have asked me to marry you if I hadn't been pregnant?'

'Vanessa, what's that—?'

'Answer me, Mitch. Would you have?'

She waited. For a long time he stared at her in silence.

'No,' he mumbled finally. 'No, Nessa. I wouldn't have.'

She nodded. Inside she was bleeding, yet somehow knowing the truth made her feel better.

'So, what's your point?' he asked.

'I wasn't trying to make a point, Mitch. I simply needed to know. For myself...'

Her stoic performance lasted only the length of time it took to climb the stairs and lock her door. Then she succumbed to an attack of old memories and an onslaught of tears.

At sixteen she'd not only been in love with Mitch; she'd imagined she'd loved him. Worse, when she'd fallen pregnant and he'd asked her to marry him, she'd assumed that meant he loved her too.

But tonight Mitch had confirmed her belief that she'd mistaken obsessive passion for love. While such a passion might be able to hold a marriage together in good times, it didn't have a snowball's chance in hell of doing it when the going got tough! And her marriage had been tough from day one and deteriorated from there!

Her father had constantly predicted as much and, even though he'd died nearly three years before she'd even suspected her marriage was in trouble, his will had been visionary. Though Brayburn was Vanessa's, the will stated that 'Mitch Randall remain manager of the property, drawing a salary of fifty per cent of any profits, until such time as my daughter divorces him.'

At the time Vanessa had laughed off the notion of divorce, saying that as her husband half of Brayburn was Mitch's anyway! And, as long as she breathed, nothing would ever be more important than being able to snuggle intimately alongside him every night for the rest of her life.

But she'd been wrong. There *were* some things more important and five years later, because of the absence of them from the relationship between herself and Mitch, the marriage was over.

At the time of the divorce Mitch's solicitor had notified her stating that Mitch not only wanted to remain as manager, but that he wanted to purchase half of Brayburn at the current market value. Her father's tears must surely have extinguished the flames of hell when *that* happened! He would never have expected that Mitch could, in just a few years, do what he'd been unable to in a lifetime—turn Brayburn into one of the five most profitable studs in the country. It was divine justice that the callous terms of his will had in fact made Mitch a wealthy man.

Vanessa could have said no to the offer, but it hadn't seemed right; Mitch's sweat was what had turned the property around and his staying on would also provide at least a token stability for Angela. She agreed to the sale only after Mitch signed a contract giving her first option should he ever decide to sell his share. It wasn't that she particularly cared for Brayburn—she'd hated it for the role it had inadvertently played in the decline of her marriage—but it was Angela's heritage, so she was determined to hang on to it until Angie was old enough to decide what she wanted to do with it.

Nowadays she realised that regardless of where she and Mitch had chosen to live they'd have ended up divorced. When you loved someone, the surroundings didn't matter; it was only when the passion of being in love faded that outside difficulties became a factor.

The ensuing days at Brayburn were an emotional trial. Constantly aware of Mitch, Vanessa was hard pressed to decide whether it was her nerves causing her the most problems or her hormones.

When she'd first moved to Perth she'd been too busy trying to regain her self-confidence, raise her daughter and establish her business to give her sexuality a thought. Then, as her life had begun to stabilise, she'd begun accepting dinner invitations from men she met in the course of her business. While she found the male company stimulating on a social level, she never experienced any desire to avail herself of it on a sexual level.

Two years ago she'd felt a moment of panic when she'd found herself questioning her sexuality. Surely thirty-three-year-old divorcees weren't supposed to accept five years of celibacy as the norm? Yet she hadn't been able to bring herself to cold-bloodedly elect to have an affair, simply to reassure herself. And in her heart she'd believed that eventually another man would come along and reawaken that aspect of her life.

Well, she'd been right! But why did the man have to be Mitch Randall—*again*?

Lightning wasn't supposed to strike twice in the same place. But it had, and her body's internal electrics were short-circuiting!

'Vanessa!'

So much for grabbing a few quiet moments of stress free time...

'I'm on the veranda, Mitch.'

He barged from the house violently, pushing his hands through the tangled length of his collar-length curls. He was showing the strain of the rapidly approaching wedding far more than Vanessa would have expected.

'Will you talk to your daughter? Every time I open my mouth she either jumps down my throat or throws herself into my arms hollering!'

Vanessa hid a half-grin. Pregnancy and bridal jitters were

proving a diabolical combination in her daughter and trying to anticipate her moods from one moment to the next would have tried even the most patient saint, let alone Mitch.

'I'm not sure I can take much more of this bloody wedding business,' he complained wearily. 'I can see why shacking up together has become so popular.'

Was the wedding the sole cause of his stress, or was the effort of maintaining the civilised façade between them as hard on him as it was her? She pushed the notion aside.

'If it's any consolation, Mitch, I think most parents probably feel like this in the final stages of a daughter's wedding,' she said. 'What's up now?'

'She's upset because I made arrangements for her and Craig to have a fully paid honeymoon on Hamilton Island! Can you tell me what's so goddamn awful about that?'

She opened her mouth to speak, but he gave her no chance.

'I mean, hell's bells, Vanessa, it's not as if I'd suggested the salt mines of Siberia! But you know what she said? "*Daddy, you're so insensitive!*"'

His deep voice trying to impersonate Angela's whine made her grin.

'*Insensitive*, mind you! What's insensitive about a man giving his daughter what he considers would be a dream honeymoon?'

'I can't imagine,' she said, fighting a smile. 'Why, not ask her yourself when she calms down a bit?'

'I would, except I'm not sure I'll be around for her *eightieth* birthday!' He dropped his body into the seat beside hers. 'God, Nessa, when did she get so temperamental?'

She raised a disbelieving eyebrow at him. 'Angela was *born* temperamental. At one stage I was convinced the "terrible twos" would last forever!'

'Judging by the last few days, you still could be right.' His 'woe is me' expression quickly changed to a reminiscent smile that softened his face and, systematically, her heart.

'Hey,' he said. 'Remember how we use to take turns walking the floor with her practically every night until she was old enough to come and climb into bed with us?'

'I'm a bit blurry on the *we* part, Mitch,' she said. 'But I remember all too clearly the feel of waking up in a wet bed and having to change the sheets at four in the morning.'

'Agh.' He groaned and pulled his Akubra over his face, but continued speaking. 'Got so bad there for a while, I was beginning to see merit in the idea of hiring her out as a proven method of birth control! And you wonder why I resorted to bathrooms and dams!'

Vanessa kept silent. No way was she going to touch that line!

He lifted his booted feet to rest them on the railing, the action drawing Vanessa's eyes to his long legs. Then, unbidden, the memory of how good it felt to have those legs wrapped around her steamed up her mind again.

'She's grown up fast.' Mitch's voice startled her from her lustful thoughts.

'Who?'

'*Angie.*'

'Oh, sorry,' Vanessa said quickly, directing her gaze in the safer direction of the horse yard. 'I was miles away.'

'I know,' came the dry response. 'Perth wasn't exactly conducive to regular weekend access.'

'I didn't me—' She decided not to bother. 'I thought she liked it there. You should have told me she didn't.'

'What would you have done if I had?'

'I don't know.' It was the truth. How would she have dealt with an ultimatum from Mitch that he'd wanted Angie to live full-time with him?

Mitch chuckled. 'Hey, Nessa, do you remember the time Angie was about three, and we went to that barbecue over at Pallisters' place?'

'Only in my worst nightmares.'

'I'll never forget how cute she looked chasing that damn pup.'

'Yeah, right through Mrs Pallister's prizewinning garden!'

'And there you and old lady Pallister were, trying to catch the pair of them. Demanding, "You get out of there this very minute, young lady!" And Angie not taking one bit of notice of either of you.'

'Then,' Vanessa interrupted, 'when she finally did come out, Mrs Pallister said Angela was the most disobedient child she'd ever met! And accused *me* of being an ineffective parent, when you, Mitch Randall, were the one who'd told Angie she could keep the puppy if she caught it!'

Mitch was unrepentant. 'Well, she'd always wanted a pup. Besides,' he said, pushing his hat back, 'I defended you both.'

'Oh, *right*!' She shot him a sceptical look. '"I'll have you know, Mrs Pallister, that my wife is a very effective parent. And Angela isn't disobedient—she's been specifically trained to ignore!" That really helped matters!'

'Stop fighting that grin, Nessa,' he teased. 'You'll get wrinkles.'

'Grandmothers are supposed to have wrinkles.'

'And grey hair, and double chins and sagging boobs—gee, Nessa, you're going to have a lot of trouble with your credibility on this.'

She laughed. 'Oh, shut up!'

'Wonder how Craig's mother will shape up?' Mitch frowned.

'We'll find out tomorrow.' Secretly she felt a tad uncomfortable about meeting Angie's future in-laws. It was stupid, but there it was.

'Angela has already instructed me that she expects us to—'

'"Make a really big impression on the O'Briens,"' she finished his sentence. 'Yeah, I know. I got the lecture too.'

'I guess that means we both have to be on our best behaviour for the next couple of days.'

'Let's just hope Angie gets a better deal with her in-laws than you did.' Vanessa wasn't making a joke, but Mitch chose to turn it into one.

'Well, at least Craig will have nothing to complain about! We're prefect.'

'Be sure and tell him that,' she smiled. 'I don't want him being ungrateful.'

'You feeling any better about him marrying Angela now?'

'Yes and no.' She expanded in reply to his interested gaze, 'I like Craig. He seems like a nice kid. And I even think he might *love* Angie rather than only be in love with her. But—'

'You think there's a difference between being in love and loving someone?'

'I know there is, Mitch. Our marriage is living proof of the fact.'

'What the hell sort of crap are you talking now?' he demanded.

'Mitch, we didn't love each other in the purest sense of the word. We were just obsessed with each other. We—'

He leapt to his feet and was instantly towering over her. His blue eyes turned storm-black and the pulse at his temple throbbed with fury. Vanessa pressed back on the chair, stunned by his sudden anger.

'I don't deny I stuffed up our marriage in a big way! But I'm not about to let you analyse, rationalise or bullshit about how *I* felt!'

Vanessa opened her mouth in protest but was too slow actually voicing it.

'I *loved* you, Vanessa!'

'If you'd loved me, *really* loved me, you'd never have considered turning to Rachel!'

'If I hadn't loved you I'd never have admitted I was tempted in the first place!' he countered.

It was a nice pat answer, but to accept it meant accepting

the old guilts she'd carried for the last ten years. That *everything* had been her fault.

'Mitch, all we had going for us was blistering hot passion. It's all we'll ever have! The other night proves that.'

'Wrong, Vanessa.' His voice had dropped to almost a whisper, 'We had love. We just didn't have faith in that love. At least, *you* didn't!'

He turned on his heel and walked to the door.

'I was wrong before,' he added. 'Craig's going to do worse than I did in the mother-in-law stakes. For all the marriages your mother had behind her, at least she was honest enough to admit that there was some good in all of them.'

Jim and Eleanor O'Brien were so nice, so friendly and so frank, that Vanessa's reaction to them ranged from relief to suicide and then murder within the first five minutes of meeting them!

'Heavens, sweetheart, you're so pretty I thought you must have been young Angela when we drove up!'

While Jim O'Brien's welcome was pure blarney, disguised in a bear-hug, she wasn't sure if Eleanor's was thinly veiled bitchiness or overt candour.

'Why, Vanessa, I love the shade of your hair. It's most becoming! Once the men are out of earshot, you must tell me which brand of dye you use.'

And it got worse!

During their first meal together, Eleanor decided it was her duty to lecture Angela and everyone else from her extensive knowledge of natural childbirth.

'I had four fine boys and not once did I have so much as an aspirin during labour,' she said proudly. Before going on to detail, in Technicolor, each of those deliveries.

'I'm sure Angela won't need any pain-killers,' Vanessa said the moment she had a chance to get a word in. 'But in the event that she does, I'm sure the doctors will be able to handle things competently.' She forced herself to smile pleasantly at Eleanor and reassuringly at her daughter. The poor kid was almost rigid with worry.

'Let's hope so!' Eleanor said heartily. 'One of my sister's girls has had nothing but problems with her back since she had her first baby! And I've no doubt it was a result of that epidural anaesthetic she had. Obviously the doctor muffed it somehow, but I ask you, why risk being paralysed to avoid a bit of pain?'

A bit of pain? A few moments ago she'd made out that natural childbirth automatically short-listed woman for sainthood!

One glance at her daughter, who looked positively comatose with terror, had Vanessa's blood boiling. She glared at Mitch. The least he could do was change the subject to football or... or something.

'Now, Angela,' Eleanor droned. 'I want you to promise you won't let those doctors force you into having any pain-killers no matter what! And, God forbid, don't believe them when if they tell you you need a Caesarean! Do you *know* how many are performed unnecessarily in this country?'

Deathly pale, Angela shook her head.

'You don't want to either!' Eleanor said. 'I've never heard of one instance in recent years where one was essential. I—'

'That's enough!' Vanessa's control exploded. 'I will not have you terrifying my daughter for another minute!'

'Nessa, honey...' Mitch whispered out of the side of his mouth as he laid a placating hand on hers.

'My dear, I never intended—' Eleanor's words were cut off by Craig.

'Shut up, Mum!' Craig interrupted. 'She's right, you're scaring Angie.'

The entire scene was enough to send Angie running from the room in tears. Craig went tearing after her and in the process managed to knock an open bottle of red wine into Mitch's lap! Mitch's reaction was a four-letter word that could make a sailor cringe.

Vanessa shut her eyes and wondered just what qualified as making 'a really big impression' in Angie's eyes.

'So,' Jim said calmly, 'how about those Broncos, uh? By the way—any more of the beef?'

'Please,' she silently pleaded. 'Let me out of here!'

'What are you doing out here?' Mitch asked from his crouched position beside a pregnant cow.

'Trying to hang on to what shred of sanity I have left and simultaneously giving my ears a rest from Eleanor's grand-motherly advice!' Mitch laughed. 'I never thought I'd say this, but I almost envy Cora.'

'Don't. Eleanor had her cornered in the study this morning double checking the double check they did yesterday on the catering.'

Vanessa groaned. The sad thing was, she knew he wasn't exaggerating. She slid from her saddle and took out the two cans of Coke she'd brought with her.

'How'd you know I was here?' Mitch asked when she handed him one.

'I didn't. I was heading down to the creek when I saw your horse. I just happened to have two drinks.'

It was true. Her sole intention had been to escape the house for a few hours alone. Why she'd altered her course when she saw Mitch's horse was something she didn't want to answer.

She nodded towards the animal lying on the ground. 'What's up? Is the calf breech?'

'Nope, but she's a maiden heifer and I don't think she's going to be able to deliver on her own.'

'You want me go get Eleanor?' Vanessa asked.

'One more suggestion like that and I'll report you to the Human Rights Commission,' he warned. 'I'm sure inflicting her on a person must be listed as an act of atrocity.'

'Hey, I thought she might give the heifer a pep-talk. You know, kind of psych her through the pain and all that.'

Mitch frowned. 'You think this poor cow hasn't got enough problems?'

Laughing, she sat down on the ground and stretched her denim-covered legs out in front of her. In the ensuing silence she covertly watched Mitch.

He was sitting on his heels and passing the can of drink from one hand to the other. Vanessa couldn't deny that, from the tip of his dusty Akubra to the soles of his equally dusty boots, Mitch Randall was the sexiest man God had ever put breath into. For a couple of days she'd felt safe believing that the attraction she felt for him was only physical. But his refusal to accept that argument had thrilled her so much, it had frightened her.

'Can I ask you, something?' His voice was hesitantly soft.

'I guess.'

'Tell me about what happened when you first arrived in Perth.' He shook his head and gave her a bewildered look. 'Why Perth?'

She could have refused. But she didn't.

'Perth wasn't my first choice. It was more like a...a last resort. I went to Sydney first—to Mum's. And,' she gave an ironic half-laugh, 'surprise, surprise, she was somewhere in Europe. I tried to get in contact with one of the girls I went to boarding school with, but she'd moved. With nowhere else to go, I jumped in a cab and got the first plane west.'

'Why? I mean, you could have contacted Cam; he was living in Sydney then.'

'Mitch, even though I considered Cam my friend, I wasn't about to land on your *brother's* doorstep and announce I'd left you! Mum's second husband lived in Perth and while they were married he and I became good friends.'

'Did I ever meet him?' Mitch's frown was typical of someone leafing through a mental photo album and trying to match faces with a string of half-forgotten names.

'No. That marriage was history by the time I met you.' She sighed. 'So's he now.'

'I'm sorry.'

'Me too. I liked him a lot. He was one of Mother's better choices.'

'When did he die?'

'He'd been dead just six months when I rang his home from Perth airport. His daughter broke down when I asked for him, then when she found out who I was she abused me with everything she could lay her tongue to.'

'Why? It wasn't your fault he and your mother broke up.' He frowned and added, 'Was it?'

She shook her head. 'I guess she had her reasons, but I wasn't emotionally equipped to handle my own problems then, let alone hers.' Vanessa took a steadying breath and met Mitch's probing eyes. 'That's when I lost it. I started crying.' She paused feeling embarrassed in retrospect. She took a long swallow of cola before continuing. God knew it was a long story!

'Next thing I knew I was sitting in the gutter, in torrential rain, and Susan Cleary was patting my shoulder and telling me everything I needed to hear: that I was an intelligent capable woman and I didn't *need* a man or anyone else to survive.'

'Cleary? Isn't that—?'

'Yeah,' she anticipated his question. 'Her daughter is going to be Angie's flower girl, so you'll get to meet her in a few days' time.'

'I can just imagine the reception I'll get,' he said drily.

'Well, I must admit she did call you some pretty colourful names, but I think it was part of her plan to stir me from self-pity to rage.' She smiled. 'I was pretty stressed out. I needed to get over all the…the physical and mental turmoil after… after what happened.'

The look Mitch gave told her he knew exactly what she was talking about…the loss of their son. She hurried on, fearing he might begin to pursue that angle again.

'Susan took me home to her place and insisted I stay until I got my head together and could find a job and a place of my own. It's hard to believe now, but there I was at twenty-five with an eight-year-old daughter and being mothered by a nineteen-year-old feminist.'

She laughed. 'Susan Cleary is the most focused and determined woman I've ever met. And I'll never be able to repay her for what she did for me.' At Mitch's questioning look she continued.

'Firstly she led me through the maze of social security red tape, then she talked me into enrolling in a course run by a local women's refuge for deserted—' She halted and darted a look at Mitch.

'A course for women who are suddenly single,' he said.

She smiled, feeling ridiculously pleased simply because he had chosen to ignore the temptation of pointing out that she hadn't fallen into the category of a 'deserted'.

'Yes.' The word was little more than a whisper and earned no response from the man opposite her. She met his eyes somewhat shyly, barely daring to breathe—though she couldn't say why—as for an interminable time they watched each other in silent scrutiny. Suddenly, sitting there in a vast paddock, beneath a cloudless blue sky, Vanessa felt as if she had the power to forge forward with her life. It was a silly sensation, for surely her life of the last ten years had been a continuously hectic battle to advancement? Yet in that instant it seemed almost as if she'd been marching in the one spot; merely marking time with her life.

'What happened then?' Mitch asked.

She could have glossed over everything and given the concise edition—indeed she probably would have a few days ago, if indeed she'd felt inclined to tell him anything; now she wanted him to know.

'The first couple of months were tough. Really tough. Mentally and financially. I couldn't get a job because I didn't have any qualifications. That was when I decided to enrol in a business management course at a local college; Susan helped organise things for me.

'When I finally found a flat I started to feel a bit more positive. Mind you,' she grinned, 'that didn't mean much! I was so utterly unprepared for the world beyond Brayburn that when I moved in and found the power turned off I rang up and abused the electricity company!'

'Well, that sounds reasonable to me,' Mitch said.

'Sure, as long as you've filed an application first!' She smiled ruefully and shook her head. 'I never knew how ill-equipped I was to deal with the real world until I left Brayburn.'

'You could have come back.' Mitch's eyes challenged her. She met his gaze.

'No, I couldn't have.' She took a sip of her drink and then rolled the can between her hands before continuing. 'I couldn't use my bank accounts because I was—'

'Afraid I'd track you down?' She nodded. 'Damn it, Vanessa, why? It wasn't as if I'd ever been violent or—'

'I was never worried about that!'

'Then what?' He shook his head. 'I don't understand…'

'I was frightened you'd demand to have Angela…I couldn't stand the thought of losing both my children.' She swallowed the lump rising in her throat and hurried on.

'I used the cheque account my mother had in both our names. She'd opened it up years ago when her third marriage failed and she took off to Europe. She called it "our emergency exit" and it was there for me to use if ever I wanted to leave Dad and Brayburn and join her or if she was ever short of funds overseas and needed to reach me in a disaster.'

'Did you manage to contact her in those first few months?'

'Susan tracked her down.'

'And did she come?'

'A failed marriage doesn't qualify as a disaster in my mother's book.'

'What do you think does?'

She shrugged. 'Who knows. She and I aren't exactly on the same wavelength when it comes to maternal responsibilities.'

'Which is why you've always been a good mother and she isn't!'

The force of Mitch's statement startled her. It also pleased her.

'Thank you,' she said. 'It means a lot that you think so, Mitch.' She met his gaze and felt so warm inside that she felt her cheeks blush. 'I have to admit, though,' she went on, 'there were times when I doubted my own ability to make decisions for myself, much less ones on Angie's behalf. I felt guilty as hell about leaving her in a daycare centre after school on the days I was late from college and couldn't pick her up from school.'

Mitch got to his feet, swearing, and hurled his drink can as if he was aiming for the horizon.

'When I think of what you went through! Damn it, Vanessa, you should have notified me!'

It was the pain in his voice that made her walk up behind him and reach for his hand.

'Mitch, you were part of my problem. Calling you wouldn't have helped,' she said gently. 'Besides, learning to stand on my own two feet was a lesson that was well overdue.'

His rough, calloused hand tightened around her much smaller, softer one and he turned to her. The sight of unshed tears in his eyes ripped at her heart. Then her own vision blurred at the tenderness in the touch of his free hand against her cheek.

'I'm sorry, Vanessa. So bloody sorry.'

She stood utterly immobile and his head descended towards her. Yet as surely as she knew the kiss was coming it still stunned her. Not because it set her blood on fire, but because it didn't. It was so childishly chaste and so sweetly given, it seemed to touch her spiritual soul.

She was still caught in its magic when he stepped away.

'I—er—guess I better check that heifer again.'

Vanessa could only nod. For the first time in a long, long time she felt soothed, rather than aroused, by Mitch's closeness. She liked the sensation of pacifying warmth every bit as much as she liked the explosive heat he could activate within her.

CHAPTER SIX

THE final days leading up to the wedding were chaotic. And made worse by Vanessa's inability to keep her thoughts free of Mitch for more than ten minutes at a time! Her mind was continually preoccupied with the memory of that sweet, honest kiss which had been laced with so much promise.

When he was out of sight she continually found herself counting down the minutes until she would see him again. And when he was around her she felt like an awkward fifteen-year-old—stammering for words and over-reacting to the least little bit of physical contact between them. And it wasn't going unnoticed!

'Give me that!' Angela attempted to grab at the antique punchbowl Vanessa was lifting from the china cabinet.

'Careful, Angie, you'll drop it!'

'I'll drop it? Now that's the pot calling the kettle black!' the teenager responded. 'At the rate you're going, Mum, my inheritance will be non-existent!'

Vanessa scowled, taking extra care holding the delicate object that had been her grandmother's.

'And at the rate *you're* going, sweet child of mine, you'll be written out of the will so it won't matter.'

'No way! Daddy'd never let you do it!' she said.

'Never let who do what?' The sound of Mitch's voice sent a tingle down Vanessa's spine and she hastily set the punchbowl on the table.

'Don't worry about it,' she said. 'Just tell your daughter to be nicer to her mother or you'll ground her on her wedding-night.'

Chuckling, Mitch surveyed the crystal sitting on the table. 'What's all this?' he frowned.

'What's left of Brayburn's heirlooms after Mum decided to help clean them.' Angela said cheekily, picking up a tray of glasses to take them to the kitchen. 'By Cora's last count, so far she's reduced my inheritance by one lamp base, one salad bowl, *three* champagne flutes—all from the one set, I might add! And a Royal Doulton cup and saucer.'

'Don't forget the set she snatched the first night she arrived,' Mitch added. 'You know, Nessa, I always thought it was only the bride and groom who suffered pre-wedding jitters, but you've blown that theory out of the water.'

Humour sparked from his deep blue eyes in the face of the lethal look Vanessa directed at him. He flashed her a wide grin and, as if he wasn't satisfied with making her belly flip-flop, followed it up with a cheeky wink that nearly buckled her knees.

The man was just too damned gorgeous for safety. Thank God she was going back to Perth in two days! It was getting harder and harder to remember that she wanted more in a relationship than just passion!

'Make yourself useful,' she told him, 'and help take this stuff through to the kitchen.'

'OK, what first?' he asked her.

'This punchbowl. Here.' She held it out to him.

As their fingers touched it was as if they somehow completed an electrical current. Simultaneously they both pulled back, then gasped in horrified unison as the ninety-year-old heirloom failed to bounce off the hard parquet floor.

'I thought you still had it.' Mitch's breath dusted her cheek.

Her pulse was racing, but that owed more, she feared, to Mitch's nearness than to what had happened.

'I thought you had it.'

'You're both as bad as each other!' Angela complained, surveying the millions of glittering fragments.

'It was an accident, honey,' Mitch said.

'Sorry,' Vanessa offered.

'Sorry!' Angela wailed. 'My child will probably be born with inherent clumsiness and you're *sorry*? It's a wonder I don't have some permanent disability, considering how many times I must have been dropped as a baby!'

Mitch looked thoughtful. 'Seven, wasn't it, Nessa?'

'Nah!' Vanessa dismissed him. 'Probably closer to eleven or twelve.'

'Course, our biggest mistake was not tanning her cute little backside more often.'

'Yes, the oversight is coming back to haunt us in the guise of an ungrateful eighteen-year-old!'

'Funny, you guys! Wait till Cora hears about this!'

They were both laughing like idiots and trying to gather up the larger pieces of glass when Cora made her presence felt in the form of a plea for divine strength.

'I'd appreciate it if you'd both stay clear of the kitchen tomorrow.'

Mitch winked conspiratorially at Vanessa.

'Well, if you're sure, Cora,' he said. 'But feel free to call on us if you feel you need any help.'

'Uh!' Cora scoffed. 'If I get *that* desperate, a Search and Destroy team will be my first choice!'

'It's your fault, you know,' Mitch accused idly over the top of his glass of cognac.

Vanessa frowned from the sofa, where she lay sprawled. It was nearly midnight and they were the only two who hadn't retired in preparation for the big day. From the elaborate sound system on the far wall the Paul McCartney lyrics provided a poetic tranquillity.

'What is?' she asked, draining her glass.

'That the punchbowl got smashed and Cora has banned us from tomorrow morning's preparations.' He grinned appreciatively. 'Smart move.'

'Don't try and pass the blame by gift-wrapping it in praise,' she said, rolling on to her side and propping herself on to one elbow.

She was feeling pleasantly relaxed as the cognac weaved its magic over her apprehension about tomorrow, but Mitch still seemed tense and edgy. His grip on the brandy balloon was tight and the cigarette in his right hand seemed almost like a life-support system. A tiny flicker of emotion sparked in her chest.

She loved it when the boyishly uncertain side of Mitch peeked out. She could count on one hand the number of times she'd seen him without his cloak of absolute self-confidence, when he'd needed her support and assurance. In the early days of their marriage the occasions had been few and far between, and non-existent following her father's death. But then, when one was trying to prove one was the best cattle man breathing, such shows of weakness would have been self defeating.

'Relax, Mitch,' she said. 'I'm nervous enough for both of us.'

'Who says I'm nervous?' he challenged.

'Me.'

'I think I'm more stunned by the speed with which everything has happened. It seems as if you both only arrived yesterday.' He looked at her. 'The four weeks have flown.'

'Yeah.' She smiled to cover the trace of regret she'd heard in her voice. 'This time tomorrow I'll have a son-in-law and twenty-four hours after that I'll be back in Perth.'

'Guess you'll be glad to get back.'

Would she? She wasn't sure. Mitch's probing gaze seemed to set off flares in her mid-section and she shifted her position, hoping to rid herself of the sensation, and hurried into speech.

'Christmas is a busy time for the boutique. We need all

hands on deck, so to speak.' Instantly her gaze sought out Mitch's strong, masculine hands. Her heart lurched. 'I... er...I'll have to find a replacement for Angie. She usually helps out during the holidays.'

She was babbling—lord knew Mitch was probably as interested in her staffing problems as he was in crochet patterns, but her hormones had gone on the rampage—*again*.

She was concentrating so hard on trying to suppress the sexual uprising within her that she didn't hear the question Mitch asked. Well, she assumed he'd asked a question, since he was looking at her expectantly as he rose from his chair.

'Uh? Er—pardon?' Her voice was a hoarse whisper as he started towards her.

'I asked if you'd like another drink?'

He was getting nearer. Another few steps and he'd hear her heart thumping. Keep him at arm's length and you'll be OK. She shoved out her arm and held her empty glass at him.

'Great idea!' She rocketed up into sitting position. 'I'll probably have to knock myself out to get any sleep tonight anyway.'

'I can think of a far better way of guaranteeing sleep.' The glass was taken from her trembling fingers. 'Eventually,' he added huskily.

It might have taken her clouded brain a split-second to comprehend the meaning of his words, but her body responded with instant heat to the burning desire in his eyes as they trailed over her. He gently took her hands in his, smiling as his fingers touched the racing pulses in both wrists.

This was not a good time for paralysis to set in, Vanessa knew, but her body wasn't paying a bit of heed to her brain and it traitorously allowed Mitch to pull her to her feet.

They stood toe to toe. His breath, with an intoxicating scent of cognac, was drugging her senses. He inched even closer until the denim of their jeans brushed.

A shiver tripped down her spine and Vanessa wasn't sure

if it was fear, excitement, erotic arousal or a combination of all three. Her gaze fixed on the strip of white enamel revealed by his slightly parted lips. She almost choked when his tongue slipped out to moisten them.

'Mitch,' she whispered. 'This is crazy.'

'Uh-uh,' he said. He dragged a hand possessively over her thigh, and had she been capable of inhaling Vanessa was sure she'd have smelt the scent of singed denim. 'This was inevitable...'

There was nothing gentle or tentative in their kiss, nor in the way their hands moved over one another. They were ex-lovers, old lovers, but they had also been first lovers and it was as if they were again, as the urgency of pent-up desire made their actions awkward and uncoordinated. Yet Vanessa didn't care. She'd spent thousands of nights trying to recapture through memory the feel of Mitch's mouth and hands against her skin, and she realised now that she'd never even come close.

The flavour of him made her blood sing and her body hum, and the duet cajoled her brain away from logic and into sensual harmony with them.

'Oh, lord, Nessa.' Mitch lifted her hair from her neck and placed a necklet of moist kisses around her throat. 'You've been driving me crazy.' His ardent ministrations continued and her head fell back to allow him more access. 'You've no idea what I've been going through...'

Didn't she? She'd practically been a walking state of arousal since she'd tended his scratches and felt the heat of his skin beneath her fingers! Automatically she once again sought to feel his powerful shoulders. The hidden strength she felt there induced her to dig her fingers into the muscular firmness.

A sensual shudder shook him and she smiled, thrilled to know she could still affect him after all this time. *Ten years*. How had she gone without this man for ten years?

Again her mouth became desperate for the flavour of his

and she forced his face back to hers and drank thirstily from it.

Just when she was certain she could no longer stand, she found herself pressed between the cool softness of the sofa and the intense heat of the only man she'd ever wanted. Her loins were pumping molten lava through her body. She hadn't felt so femininely alive for what seemed like a hundred years!

Looking into the handsome face of the man lying half across her, she saw that the flaming desire in the blue of his eyes could not only match hers, but satisfy it too.

He poked a finger between two buttons on her blouse and instinctively she arched into him, her breathing ragged.

'Not in a hurry, are you, Nessa?' he asked, torturing her with a slow, seductive grin. One button was freed.

This tempt-and-tease routine was one they'd played a dozen times before. Her body was on fire and it took every ounce of willpower she had to not push his fingers aside and take over the task.

'No,' she lied as a second button surrendered to him.

He leaned close and flicked his tongue from the base of her throat to the top of her cleavage. The middle button of the blouse opened and he pressed a heated palm against the thin lace of her teddy. Her stomach muscles contracted and she bit her lip to keep from groaning.

His chuckle was as angelic as Satan's. 'Feel free to wave the white flag any time.'

'Sorry. Don't have one.' In one fluid motion she managed to grab the front of his shirt with one hand and cup the front of his jeans with the other. He pressed into her hand; his choked gasp was a mix of frustration and release.

'Not in a hurry, are you?' she questioned, pulling his shirt free of his pants and sliding one finger into the waistband.

His body bucked instantly and he grasped her wrists. The sudden reaction stunned her and she found herself with both arms stretched above her head. Focusing solely on her eyes, and with slow deliberation, he straddled her hips. Even through the denim of their jeans, his hardness pressed into her and Vanessa's pleading whimper was as uncontrollable as the way her lower body rose from the sofa to bring them closer.

Her actions forced his head to drop back and his eyes to close. The expression revealed his inner battle to balance his eagerness to bring this coupling to its natural conclusion with his efforts for restraint.

After an instant he eased away from her transferring his weight to his knees.

For several seconds they simply stared at each other. The only sound was the unsteady panting as each of them breathed. Then Mitch altered his hold on her hands so that one of his was free and, without taking his gaze from her eyes, he started to undo the remaining buttons of her blouse.

Each time his fingers brushed against the fine lace of the red teddy she wore, thousands of miniature butterflies danced in her stomach, making her body flinch in delight. Her responses brought a smile to the masculine mouth that in the past had given her so much pleasure. Erotic memories of things she and Mitch had shared threatened to stop her lungs functioning and she forced herself to heave in a huge breath for fear she'd suffocate.

When all the buttons were undone, Mitch trailed a less than steady finger from between her breasts and down over her belly to the snap of her jeans. Her heart skidded and desire cramped her womb.

'Not exactly what one imagines an expectant granny to be wearing,' he said huskily before peeling the blouse wide and exposing her scantily clad body. With her arms pinned above her head there was no way she could impede his view and she was self-consciously aware that the gossamer fine lace of her teddy did nothing to conceal the aroused rigidity of her nipples.

'Oh, lord, Nessa,' he whispered on a half-breath. 'You're more beautiful than ever.'

The adoration in his voice thrilled her. Then the delicious gentleness with which he suckled each hardened peak through the lace wiped all logical thought from her mind. Nothing mattered save the fact that she was back in the arms of a man her body had craved, and been denied, for just on a decade.

The dispersal of their remaining clothes was accomplished while Vanessa hovered above reality in an erotic cloud, and she was only dimly aware of Mitch manoeuvring them to the floor. But her eyes flew open and her body bucked in response to his whisper-soft touch the moment his hand stroked between her thighs.

She arched into him, driven by the knowledge of bygone memories and an all-consuming need to once again let Mitch show her heaven on earth.

'Oh, Mitch…'

'Easy, honey,' he whispered, delivering a butterfly-light kiss to her throat. 'I'm flat-out keeping this train on the rails as it is.'

Through passion-heavy eyes, Vanessa saw the truth of his words in the strain on his face. Darling Mitch. In their youth he'd never allowed the urgency of his own pleasure to override hers, and her heart flipped at the knowledge that even after all these years he was still prepared to turn himself inside out to ensure she too experienced the ultimate erotic glory with him. But as far as she could see right now, patience was torturous not virtuous!

'Mitch.' She smiled, slipping a hand between them to take possession of him. 'I think it's time I took over the throttle.'

When she guided him into her his strangled groan of relief was in harmony with her own and their climb to mankind's sensual Everest was made as one, their bodies and breathing in perfect unison.

Nothing had changed between them on this level. Nothing. It was as if they'd been created for each other.

The sound of a whistling kettle tugged Vanessa from sleep, but determinedly she fought to ignore it. Right now she wanted to drain every drop of reality from her dream of being in Mitch's arms again. She squeezed her eyes tight against the shrill of the kettle as if doing so would somehow dim her hearing and tried to hang on to a dream so real she could feel Mitch's breath against her neck...feel the weight of his leg across hers...

The kettle stopped and Vanessa rolled over on to—

Her eyes flew open and she barely managed to cut off her scream before it left her throat.

Oh, God! It wasn't a dream! Mitch was sleeping alongside her! OK, it was half a dream—they weren't in her bed. They were both stark naked and lying on the floor of the family-room! Good God, anyone might have walked in! Cora, Angie—*Angie*!

Horror spurred Vanessa to violent life and she gave Mitch a vicious thump on the shoulder at the same instant she kicked his leg off her.

'What the—?'

She didn't give him a chance to conquer his sleep-heavy confusion.

'Get up! And for God's sake get dressed!' she hissed as she flung his rumpled shirt at him.

'I've got a better idea,' he grinned, lunging at her kneeling form. 'Let's not.'

In an easy motion he pulled her across him and tried to muffle her protest with his mouth. Vanessa swore and furiously began tossing her head. 'Snap out of it, Mitch! You're being crazy!'

He chuckled. 'You said that last night too and look how great that turned out.'

'Mitch! Stop it!'

His hands stilled and the teasing light left his face as if he'd only now grasped the urgency in her voice.

'You regret last night?'

'No! Of course—I mean *yes*! No! Oh, I don't know! It's not important.'

'It is to me, Vanessa.'

His eyes were a sea of hope. Did that mean that he wanted to…that perhaps…? Oh, stop it, Vanessa! You're being an idiot! Heavens, they didn't have time for a post-mortem!

'Let me up, Mitch; we have to get dressed.'

'What's the hurry?' he asked, sinking back on to one elbow and propping up his head as he gave her nakedness a very thorough and indolent once over. 'No one will be up for at least another hour.'

'Cora's already up,' she said, pulling on the discarded teddy from the night before. Great, one strap was broken!

'Damn, but you're sexy in that thing!' He grinned. 'You're even sexier out of it.'

Ignoring him, she worked her arms into her blouse.

'OK, Nessa, let's have it. What's your problem?'

'My problem *is* that in a little over three hours people are going to start arriving expecting to see the parents of the bride dressed in more than their birthday suits!' Mitch's jaw dropped open. 'And I intend to see that at least fifty per cent of their expectations are met!'

'Stone the crows!' Mitch leapt to his feet. 'The bloody wedding clear slipped my mind!'

'Yeah, well, let's hope we can *slip* up the stairs and into our rooms just as easily,' Vanessa said drily. 'All we need is to run into Cora or Angie!'

'So long as we're dressed, where's the problem?' Mitch sounded genuinely puzzled by her concern and Vanessa swung her gaze to him in disbelief.

'Mitch, even someone who was brain-dead could work out

exactly what went on last night given our appearance and the fact that neither of our beds have been slept in.'

'So?' He was smirking like a nymphomaniac in a male prison. 'Lots of parents probably celebrate their offspring's marriage with a night of wild unfettered lovemaking.'

'Perhaps. But in case you've forgotten, Mitch, *we're divorced.*'

How she managed to cope with the seventeen thousand minor disasters which occurred that morning Vanessa didn't know. All she had been aware of was the shrill of the kettle resounding through her head. Now, standing in the front row of the assembled crowd with her knees threatening to buckle and her vision misted by tears, she forced herself to forsake her introspection and remember this was her daughter's day.

When first chords of the Bridal March were struck she pasted on a smile and turned to await the bridal party.

The first to appear was the flower girl, Kassie Cleary. The flaxen-haired three-year-old was a giggling bundle of rose-clad nerves and a delightful contrast to the rigid, tearful bridesmaid who followed her. When the two attendants were halfway down the length of red carpet dividing the guests of the bride and groom, Angela and Mitch came into view.

Vanessa swallowed a sob at the sight of her beautiful raven-haired daughter on the arm of the man who'd fathered her. They were so alike. So tall and strong and so much a part of her heart. She watched Angela's apprehensive expression change into a smothered chuckle at something; Mitch whispered to her and the pair exchanged a loving look. Vanessa felt her heart pinch for all the time they'd missed together.

The instant Mitch's lightning-like gaze met hers her heartbeat went haywire and the hard drive in her brain collapsed. She was unable to process a single image other than last night, or recall the feel of anything but the gentle strength of Mitch's touch.

He winked, returning normal programming to her body, before muttering something out of the side of his mouth to his daughter. Angie seemed to lose stride, but with her father's guidance she quickly recovered and sent a beaming smile towards Vanessa.

When they reached the arch of bougainvillaea where Father Fitzgerald stood, Craig stepped forward and extended his hand towards his future wife.

'O'Brien,' Mitch said in a 'hushed' voice audible, Vanessa suspected, to only the first five rows on both sides! 'You cause my little girl one skerrick of disappointment and I'll use you for target practise.'

'*Daddy*!'

Angie's hissed protest was ignored by everyone as Craig looked Mitch straight in the eye.

'If I do, sir, I'll load the gun myself.'

Slowly Mitch's face relaxed into a smile and Vanessa exhaled a heartfelt sigh as he placed Angie's hand in that of the younger man's. Then, after giving his daughter a quick kiss on the cheek, he moved to the chair beside Vanessa.

'How'd we look, uh?' he asked.

'W-w-w-wonderful,' she said, trying to mop two wayward tears without smudging her eyeliner and mascara.

'We were both scared witless.' His smile was sheepish. 'Did it show?'

She shook her head. 'No, you…you both looked beautiful.'

Mitch's slow, admiring appraisal of her again affected the tempo of her heart. At this rate she'd be a candidate for a coronary care unit before the service was over!

'Reckon we both come a poor second to you,' he whispered.

The priest welcomed everyone and from that point onwards Vanessa struggled to keep her mind from the memories of a similar event nineteen years ago.

With the religious part of the day over, the guests were availing themselves of the copious quantities of food and drink set out in the huge organza-lined white marquee. The photographer had finished taking the official photos over an hour ago, but Vanessa still hadn't been able to shake Mitch from her side.

His constant presence, not to mention his pseudo-innocuous contact with her body, was driving her out of her mind. Short of forcibly shrugging free of the hold he kept on her elbow as they mingled and chatted with the guests, there didn't appear anyway she could convince him to leave her alone. She was about to fall back on the old 'I have to use the bathroom' excuse when Mitch's brother Cam injected himself between them.

'Well done, you pair!' he congratulated. 'As wedding ceremonies go, that one was pretty good!'

'Coming from a man who equates marriage with castration, that statement lacks credibility,' Mitch teased.

'Hey, everyone is saying so! Besides, it's only the thought of my own castration that causes me problem.'

Someone called Vanessa from behind and all three of them turned. Cam gave a subdued whistle as a stunning platinum blonde approached them.

'Down, boy!' Vanessa laughed. 'Susan Cleary is *not* your type.'

'Vanessa.' Mitch frowned. 'Any female with a pulse is Cam's type.'

'No one would guess from this shindig that you were against this marriage,' Susan said in her familiar husky tones.

'Good.' Vanessa smiled. 'I'm not sure I am any more.'

She exchanged a hug and a kiss with the younger woman before stepping back and introducing her to Mitch and his brother. Cam, for the first time Vanessa could recall, seemed dumbstruck. Mitch looked uncomfortable.

'Well, Mitch, I meet you at last.' Susan extended her hand.

'Although I probably know more about you than you know yourself—'

'And you no doubt think I'm a prize bastard.'

Susan smiled. 'I think *all* men are bastards.'

Vanessa couldn't hide a grin as both males actually flinched at Susan's honesty. Mitch recovered first.

'In that case I won't take personal offence. Besides, I'll always be grateful for the way you helped Vanessa and Angela all those years ago.'

'Vanessa did it herself. I just gave her a shoulder when she needed one.'

'So, Susan—' Cam turned on the megawatt smile that was both his trademark and a lethal weapon where females were concerned and Mitch sent Vanessa a look that said, 'Let's see Ms All-Men-Are-Bastards withstand this' '—I hear the bridesmaid is your daughter. I'm not sure I've met your husband.'

'I'm sure you haven't, since I'm not married.'

Cam made no attempt to conceal the fact that the comment pleased him. 'Does that mean I can have the pleasure of a dance later?'

'No. It means I'm not married. Excuse me, Mitch, Vanessa. I'll just go and make sure my darling daughter isn't doing anything she shouldn't.'

'Is doing things one shouldn't a common trait with the women in your family, Susan?' Cam enquired suavely.

'No, but evidently thick-headedness seems to run through the male Randalls.' After a speaking glance at Mitch, Susan left.

'Oh, God, Vanessa,' Cam gasped. 'I'm in love.'

'You're wasting your time, Cameron. Susan Cleary isn't interested in your type.'

'You mean she's gay?'

Vanessa shook her head. 'Nope. Just smart.'

'She's also right about Randall men being thick-headed,'

Mitch added removing the glass of champagne and orange from Vanessa's hand. 'Dance with me.'

'No, I...' The touch of his hand against the exposed skin of her shoulder choked off her words.

'It's the bridal waltz. It's expected.' The collage of feeling in his eyes caused more confusion to Vanessa's already tremulous emotions. But, being aware of the danger of trying to interpret the feelings of either one of them, Vanessa quickly turned her gaze. Sure enough, Craig was leading Angela on to the portable dance-floor.

Great! She was trapped. Sudden heart failure was about the only good excuse Angie would accept for her mother sitting out the bridal waltz.

When the air filled with the introductory bars of 'Can I Have This Dance?' Vanessa's senses reeled so wildly that for an instant she thought she really would collapse! How utterly bizarre that Angie should have chosen that particular song! Though grateful for the firm guiding arm of the man at her side, she didn't trust herself to look and see if he'd recognised the music as that which had been *their* bridal waltz.

'Nessa?'

She bit her lip and managed a nod in response and allowed herself to be led toward the dance-floor. Silently praying for the day to be over.

'Think we can remember how to do this?'

Mitch's gently spoken question coincided with his hands going to her waist and him lifting her up the six-inch step on to the polished dance-floor. His touch burned right through her, and when her feet were again on the floor her vision had deteriorated to the extent where Mitch's face was the only thing in clear focus.

Their eyes locked as they took the minuscule steps necessary to bring them into the waltz position. For a moment they assumed the correct dancing position, but within seconds the pretence of dancing was overshadowed by the need for physical contact. The space between them shrank to nothing and they were so close, Vanessa feared the wild thumping of her heart might knock Mitch to the other side of the dance-floor.

The scent of him invaded her nostrils and, working with the heady feel of his muscular thighs against hers and the sheer bliss of his palm on her bare back, incited a riot in her loins. She moved her hands up his chest to link in the dark curls brushing the back of his collar and pressed herself into his body.

His half-muffled groan sounded almost relieved as it feathered past her ear. She lifted her head to look at him and they held each other's gaze for several seconds before their bodies trembled in unison. She watched as his head started to lower and could no more have turned from his kiss than stopped the sun from sinking. It was short, wet and invasive, and it ended too quickly. She sighed her regret and rested her forehead against the front of his shirt.

At some point their feet stopped moving and it was only the sway of their bodies that might possibly have fooled onlookers into believing they were doing anything as innocuous as dancing when in fact they were making mental love to one another.

'Nessa, open your eyes. Look at me.' Mitch's words were husky with need.

'I can't.' Her voice was scarcely audible to her own ears, yet even as she said the words she raised her head and looked at him.

Without breaking eye-contact Mitch moved one hand to the curve of her lower back and lifted the other to the back of her neck, to slide his thumb beneath the choker-line neckline of her dress. Then with an incisively seductive rhythm he began stroking it in and out. Over and over.

It was only the support of his hand on the back of her neck that prevented her head from lolling back in blissful abandon. And it was pure erotic desire that lead her to slip her own finger into the V of his shirt and begin caressing the edge of his collarbone in perfect tempo with his touch. Her body absorbed the silent moan that shook him and she had to close her eyes against the threat of tears.

'Ah, Nessa. Don't go back to Perth tomorrow. Stay here.'

'I…I can't.'

'Please? Stay with me for just a few days. For—'

'No, Mitch.'

'Please, I—'

Their token efforts to appear to be dancing were knocked aside when a smiling Cam and his three-year-old partner barrelled into them.

'Damn it, Cam!' Mitch snapped, quickly releasing Vanessa to confront his brother. 'Can't you watch what you're doing?'

'What's eating you?'

While Cam was clearly stunned by his brother's overreaction, Vanessa's brain told her the interruption was a godsend. She took the opportunity to free herself from Mitch's embrace.

'Sorry, Cam. My fault, I wasn't concentrating on where I was putting my feet,' Mitch said, moving to draw Vanessa back into his arms.

'Excuse me,' she said, smiling unsteadily and running nervous hands over her dress. 'I…I have to go and check some things.'

'They can wait,' Mitch said, the desire in his eyes mirroring her own feelings so acutely that for a fleeting second she almost surrendered to the raw, unsatisfied need coursing through her body. Almost.

'No. They…can't. I'm sorry.'

'Vanessa…' He reached to grasp her hand, but she recoiled from his touch, uncaring of Cam's curious look.

'No, no. There are…things. I…' Knowing she sounded as incoherent as she felt, she fought to pull herself together.

'There are things that need my attention. I...I'll see you both later.'

Fortunately none of the guests considered it unduly strange that the mother of the bride should flee to the house with tears streaming down her face.

CHAPTER SEVEN

IT WAS nearly ten-thirty p.m. when Vanessa let herself into her unit. Dropping her keys on the telephone table, she flicked the answering machine to rewind and walked into the kitchen. With mechanical precision she dumped her handbag and groceries on the breakfast bar, switched on the kettle then slumped on to a stool and kicked off her shoes before giving her attention to the mail she held.

Apart from a postcard from Susan claiming Vanessa had missed the opportunity of a lifetime by not joining her at week-long seminar on 'Single Women—Happy By Choice', nothing else was of sufficient interest to waylay her from a refreshing shower and bed.

When the kettle whistled she made herself a cup of herbal tea which professed to be a 'soothing remedy guaranteed to invoke restful sleep'. Ha! she thought, carrying the cup into her bedroom. She'd been drinking copious quantities of the stuff for weeks now and it wasn't doing a damn bit of good! Sleep had become a pipe dream for her these days, despite the fact that she was always achingly tired after working twelve-hour days.

She might have been able to blame Perth's heatwave conditions for her discomfort, except that they'd only been in evidence the last week and besides, the air-conditioner in her bedroom was blissfully cool. No the sole reason she'd had trouble sleeping since her return from Brayburn nearly five weeks ago, was the constant invasion of Mitch Randall into her dreams. Into her nights, into her days, into her soul!

Surely to God it couldn't last much longer. Could it?

She was stripped naked and adjusting the water temperature in the shower when the phone rang. She decided to let the machine pick up the call, but the insistent ringing reminded her that she'd switched it off. Not bothering with a towel, she ran to answer it.

'Hello?'

'Vanessa.' A flame leaped from her loins and burned at her heart. 'This is Mitch.'

Glancing down at her now alert nipples and wanting to cry, she sagged against the ridged coarseness of the wallpaper. Damn the man! Damn him for the effect he had on her body and on her mind!

'Vanessa? Vanessa, are you there?'

'I'm here,' she muttered through gritted teeth. 'What are you doing calling so late?'

'I'm calling *again*, because you haven't responded to the half-dozen messages I've left on your machine.'

'What? I don't...' Suddenly the fog lifted from her brain. 'I'm sorry, I didn't get around to playing the messages.'

'Oh? And what is it that's left you so breathless and short of time?'

The implications of his question made her furious!

'It just so happens I was about to get under the shower! If I sound breathless it's because I had to sprint to the phone when it became obvious the caller wasn't giving up! Now do you want to tell me why you called?'

'I'm not sure.' His tone was weary and she listened to several seconds of transcontinental silence before he spoke again. 'Angie asked me not to tell you, but...'

Panic enveloped her mind and carried to her voice. 'Mitch, what is it? What's wrong?'

'The doctor said it's nothing to worry about—'

'*The doctor*! Is it the baby? My God, Mitch, what's happ—'

'Damn! I knew this was how you'd react.'

'For God's sake, Mitch, *tell* me what's wrong!'

'Angie went into premature labour a few hours ago—'

'Oh, no!' She sank to her knees, the phone dropping to her shoulder as she clasped an arm across her stomach. Nausea and fear gripped her with vicelike tenacity. Oh, no. Don't let Angie lose her baby. Please God...

'Vanessa, sweetheart, please talk to me. Nessa! Nessa!'

Mitch's frantic pleas seemed distant and it was more the need to hear his voice clearly again, rather than logic, that made her put the receiver back to her ear.

'Mitch...'

'Oh, thank God!' The relief in his voice was fervent. 'Honey, are you OK?'

'I...I think so. I'm not...not sure.' She fought to keep her voice steady and brain controlled. 'Tell me the truth. Is Angela OK?'

'She's fine.'

'Really?' Tears were running down her face and she was trembling from head to toe.

'Honestly. The doctor has stopped her labour and he doesn't expect it to start again.'

'And if it does?'

'Then they'll try and hold it off again. The doctor—'

'What if they can't hold it off, Mitch? What then? What chance do they give the baby?'

'Vanessa—' his tone was soothing and caring '—the doctor doesn't think there's going to be a problem. He's told Angie and Craig that if the medication continues to be effective they'll probably let her home at the end of next week.'

'Home! My God, are they crazy? Mitch, you can't let them send her home. You can't—'

'Calm down, honey,' he said gently. 'Your falling apart isn't going to do anyone any good. True?'

She nodded at his reasoning, then, realising he couldn't see her, said, 'Yes. OK, you're right. I'm c-c-c-calm.'

He gave a soft chuckle. 'I'm not quite convinced.'

She felt a half-smile stretch through her tear-washed face. 'Me, neither,' she confessed. 'But, I'm working on it. It…it's just that I know how she'd feel if anything happened to…to…'

'I know.' There was a long silence as neither spoke. 'Angie was worried you'd react like this. That's why she didn't want me to tell you.'

Vanessa wanted to simultaneously choke her daughter for wanting to keep this from her and hug her until she was safely delivered into motherhood. She could do neither from Perth.

'What hospital is she in? Tamworth?'

'Yeah. I'm staying in town so I'll be seeing her first thing tomorrow morning. Any message for her?'

'Yes,' Vanessa said forcing a smile into her voice. 'You can tell her that grandmothers expect to be told *everything*. And that she'd better not try keeping any details from me when I arrive tomorrow!'

Mitch swore. 'Vanessa, you're in no emotional state to fly over now. You hate flying at the best of times. Besides, it's after midnight.'

'Not on this side of the country. If I hurry I can still make the last flight across to Sydney tonight.'

'Vanessa, that's stupid.'

'Too bad. I'm still doing it.' She anticipated the exaggerated sigh that met her ear. 'Mitch?'

'What?'

'Tell Angie I'll see her sometime tomorrow afternoon. And…thanks for calling me.'

Sleeping on a plane was as foreign to Vanessa as shoes were to a fish. So while other passengers on the eleven thirty-five p.m. flight from the west appeared relatively bright-eyed when they disembarked at a rain-lashed Mascot airport at six-forty a.m. the following morning, Vanessa didn't need her compact mirror to tell her she looked like one of the walking dead.

She made her way to the luggage carousel grateful that, unlike her black silk shirt, her Levi 501s were too tight to wrinkle and that, given her fifties-style pony-tail and flatties, the worst thing people would think was that she was making some sort of retro fashion statement. Six hours ago, dressing to impress had been the last thing on her mind, and it showed! Shoving an errant strand of hair behind her ear, she waited for her bags to appear while mentally calculating her next step.

First she'd have to check which airline had the first available flight to Tamworth, then purchase a ticket and call the hospital. She spied her bags and, as they rotated towards her, shrugged her shoulder-bag into a more comfortable position and bent to snatch them from the moving belt.

'I'd know that butt anywhere! Even *with* jeans on.'

Vanessa spun around so quickly that she overbalanced, and had it not been for two firm male hands which quickly steadied her she'd have landed on the carousel. She knew she looked totally stunned, but then she *was*.

'Mitch!'

'Right first go,' he congratulated her with a broad grin as he released her.

She blinked three times to clear her head, then watched with muted fascination as the best looking male in the terminal—oh, all right, the world—snared her two pieces of luggage and placed them at her feet.

'Lord, Nessa! What have you got in here?'

'Never mind that. What are *you* doing here?'

'I knew you'd be in no mental shape to hop on another plane to Tamworth, so I decided to drive down and meet you.' he reached out and brushed his thumbs under her eyes, looking concerned. 'Though, at the risk of getting a smack in the mouth, I've gotta say that physically you don't look too hot either.'

'Physically I feel like hell, so I'll put a rain-check on the backhander.' She tried for a smile, but knew it was a weak one. Then again, that was exactly how she always seemed to feel around Mitch these days. 'How's Angie?'

'Relax. I phoned the hospital about thirty minutes ago.' He picked up her bags with a theatrical grimace. 'Our daughter is doing fine and so's the baby.'

Vanessa sighed with relief. 'Thank God.'

'On the other hand, our recently acquired son-in-law is a mental wreck and when I last saw him six hours ago the black rings under *his* eyes put yours in the non-existent category.'

'Gee, Mitch, I'm glad I'm not the only one you lavish flattery on.'

He motioned her towards the exit, but she didn't budge.

'I'm not going anywhere until I get some decent coffee and food into me. I can't eat on planes and I'm starving.'

'Reckoned you would be,' Mitch said. 'So I've booked a room at the Airport Hilton and ordered breakfast for seven-fifteen.'

She wondered if the excited response in her abdomen was due to her ravenous state or his smile, which seemed powerful enough to short-circuit the entire airport electrical system.

'You interested?'

Her hormones ran amok at his careless choice of words and for a second she forgot that the subject of discussion was *food*. Heavens, her resistance to Mitch was declining with every trip over here!

'Vanessa?' He pulled her from her dazed thoughts, his next words indicating he'd interpreted her silence as scepticism. 'There's no sinister motive behind booking the hotel. I just thought you might want to shower and take a nap before we head north. It's your call—you want to hit the Hilton or the coffee shop?'

She glanced out of the huge glass doors at Sydney's wet grey morning and thought how ironic that an airport and rain should again be the back drop for a dramatic emotional occurrence. Except this time she wasn't falling apart. This time she was falling in love...again.

'Mmm,' Vanessa sighed. 'This is the best breakfast I've had in a hundred years.'

'I guessed. Not too many women would put away a bowl of cereal, a double serving of bacon and eggs, a glass of pine-apple juice, three cups of coffee and still have the strength to polish off an apple.' From across the table Mitch's voice was thick with amusement.

'I warned you I was starving. Yesterday I skipped lunch, missed dinner last night and by the time I left the boutique and grabbed some groceries it was ten o'clock. After talking to you it was all I could do to shower, chuck some clothes together and drive to the airport in time to make the plane.'

Mitch frowned. 'You always work such long days?'

'I have recently. Not having Angela to consider, I tend to be more flexible about mealtimes.'

'Is it really necessary to devote so much time to work, though? It's not good for your health.'

'That from a man who spends fourteen hours a day doing heavy physical labour?'

Mitch twisted his mouth as if he were trying to stop a barbed comment and his obvious reluctance to get into an argument made Vanessa want to kick herself.

'I *used* to work fourteen-hour days,' he said finally. 'But a few years back I learned to delegate. You should try it.'

'Can't. I'm trying to swing a deal with a French couturier to market his range in Australia. If it comes off it'll be a major coup for the store.' She shook her head. 'If not, I won't have anyone to blame but myself.'

'Sounds like you're doing well.'

'I am. Standing Alone is regarded as one of Western Australia's most exclusive stores.' She didn't try to conceal the pride she felt, because she'd had to battle hard for her success—physically and financially. She hadn't used one cent of her income from Brayburn.

'Somehow I wasn't all that surprised when I heard what you'd called it.' His tone was self-reproachful. 'I don't imagine the inspiration came solely from the fact you carry one-off stuff.'

'I do not carry *stuff*,' she said, softening her prim tone with a smile. 'But you're right, for me the name was representative of my need to be independent.'

'From me?'

She considered his question. Once she'd have said yes right off. Now she knew her reasons had been far more complicated.

'Not really.' His surprise at her reply was evident. 'I think, rather than needing to be independent *from* you or from Brayburn, or—' she gave an ironic grimace '—from the suffocating lack of faith my father showed in my judgement, I needed to be independent *for me*. I needed more to prove myself to me than to anyone else.'

'And have you?'

She smiled. 'I like to think so.'

'Are you happy?'

'Happy?' she echoed dumbly, all ability to think coherently evaporating as he lifted her hand and turned it palm upwards.

'Yeah, you know—happy with your life.'

He was watching her so intently that she was sure he could read her mind. That was OK: right now with his finger tracing the network of tiny veins on the back of her wrists, it was blank anyway. But her heart wasn't. And, if he suddenly gained an insight into that, she was in big, big trouble! Reluctantly she tugged her hand away and stood up.

'I will be once I've had a shower and changed my clothes.' She was determined to keep things light. 'And I'll be ecstatic once I see Angela and know she's OK.'

They both knew she'd skirted the question, but Vanessa hoped she was the only one who knew why.

'Right, then.' He picked up the newspaper and stood up. 'You hit the shower and I'll stretch out with the crossword until you're ready.'

'Crossword?' She laughed. 'Mitch, you *hate* crosswords! You used to whinge because I spent so much time doing them.'

'Yeah, well, living alone, I had to find something to do to fill my evenings. Besides—' his eyes hardened '—it wasn't that I actually hated crosswords, I just hated having to *compete* with them.'

Vanessa met his accusing glance, intending to stare him down, but surprisingly he turned away almost immediately.

'Better get a move on,' he said, flopping down on to the bed. 'We've got over five hours of driving ahead of us.'

It wasn't until she'd finished marvelling just how good a hot shower could feel that it dawned on Vanessa that, since Tamworth was a solid six-hour drive from Sydney, and Mitch had been here to meet her plane, he must have left right after he'd finished calling her last night! He wasn't going to be in any condition to turn around and drive straight back—he had to be even more tired than she was! While on paper her flight appeared to take six hours, allowing for the difference in time zones, she'd only been in the air four. Mitch on the other hand had been behind the wheel of the four by four for six, long, dark hours.

Pulling on an oversized yellow T-shirt emblazoned with 'Life is Short', Vanessa decided that letting a fatigued man get behind the wheel in these atrocious weather conditions was one way of making it even shorter! While she'd hoped to make Tamworth hospital by mid-afternoon, she didn't want to achieve it on a *stretcher*!

After giving her hair a good brush, she pulled it back and began braiding it. The smart thing to do was catch four or five hours' sleep, have a light lunch and start out just after midday. Of course, Mitch wouldn't be receptive to the idea. That was one of Mitch's biggest failings—he always thought he was the only one entitled to make decisions. Well, Vanessa had been making her own for ten years and if Mitch Randall thought she was going to backslide into the unchallenging, docile, obedient person she'd been when they were married he could think again!

If he insisted on leaving right away, then fine—he could go by himself! But she was going to call the hospital and tell Angie there'd been a change of plan and not to expect her until about six that evening.

She zipped her make-up bag closed and with a determined glance at her reflection strode from the bathroom.

'Mitch, I don't care what you...' The words died on her lips at the sight of six plus feet of masculinity stretched out on the bed.

The pen had slipped from his fingers and fallen on to the crossword he'd been doing. Kneeling on the vacant side of the bed, she picked it up and scanned his efforts. He'd completed five clues. She frowned at his answer to a four-letter word for 'nuisance'—'wife'.

'Cute, mate, but it just so happens the four-letter word is "pest",' she muttered testily.

Beneath her the mattress rolled and pitched her forward across him; a vicelike arm held her there.

'Ah, I must have confused it with the six-letter one—"ex-wife".'

His teasing grin had no effect on her. The feel of him did.

'Let me up,' she demanded, stunned when he immediately released her. She'd expected, or perhaps 'hoped' was the correct word in this case—that he would refuse.

'You ready to leave?' he asked.

'No!' she snapped, knowing she sounded unreasonably angry, but unable to help herself. 'You're not in any condition to drive and I'm not going to run the risk of getting killed in an accident because you fall asleep at the wheel! I think it would be far wiser if we waited until about midday. Now if you—'

'Great idea,' he agreed. 'Wake me when you're ready. I'm bushed.' He rolled on to his side and left her facing his broad muscular back.

She stared mutely at his horizontal form, wondering why he wasn't arguing with her. It wasn't like Mitch to want to waste daylight hours sleeping.

'Wake you? But what if I want to go to sleep?'

'Then go to sleep.'

'There's only one bed and if you think I'm crawling into it with—'

'Right now my need for sleep overrides my need for sex, but if you don't trust me feel free to take the sofa.'

'Why should I have to take the sofa?'

'Jeez!' He rolled back and glared at her. 'OK, OK—I'll take the sofa! Will that make you happy?'

She looked at the small piece of furniture and knew that it wouldn't comfortably accommodate Mitch's huge frame.

'No, don't bother. I guess we can sleep head to toe.'

'Head to toe?' He gave an incredulous laugh. 'If that's what you want fine. Only *please* let me get some sleep.'

'Fine! I will! But can you set the radio alarm first? I always mess those things up.'

'Phone reception and have them put a wake-up call through.'

'Well, what time should I get them to call?'

'You decide, Nessa. Whatever you like.'

His voice was flat and bored, as if he were speaking to a particularly persistent child.

'I thought if we left here about twelve-thirty we—'

'Terrific. Good choice. Twelve-thirty is fine. Now shut up and let me get some rest.'

What she really wanted to do was hit him on the head with

the bedside lamp and send him to his eternal rest! Instead, she snatched up the telephone and buzzed Reception.

Driving rain flogged the windscreen as they passed Vanessa's old boarding school on the northern outskirts of Maitland. There'd been no respite from the foul weather in the two and a half hours since they'd left the hotel. It had been bad enough on the multi-lane divided expressway, but the condition of the less salubrious New England Highway had to be stretching Mitch's concentration to the limit.

'Want to stop for coffee?' she asked, spying a service station up ahead.

'There's a McDonald's about thirty minutes up the road. Think you can hold off till then?' Mitch spared her only a quick glance.

'Sure. I thought you might be getting a bit weary.'

He smiled. 'I am, but I'm good for another half-hour.' Again he darted a look to Vanessa. 'We'll call Angie, too. She'll be worried knowing we're driving in this.'

'Not half as worried as I'd have been flying through this.' She turned a little in the seat and pulled her legs up under her, glad she'd opted for the comfort of the Lycra biking shorts she wore over her usual penchant for tailored trousers. 'I want you to know I really appreciate your driving all this way to get me.'

'It's no big deal.'

'It is to me. I know how much you hate spending time away from Brayburn and—'

'Vanessa, if I can accept that you've changed, why the hell won't you believe that I have, huh?' Mitch asked with obvious irritation. 'And has it ever once entered your head that maybe my former *apparent* obsession with the property was more a misconception on your part than reality?'

'Perhaps you have changed, Mitch,' she conceded. 'But I

didn't imagine all those lonely hours I spent sitting around the house waiting for you to come home.'

He gave her a look that seared her senses. It was just a look, yet her stomach was cartwheeling and her heart was pumping blood so fast Vanessa figured it had set a world speed record. She spun her head towards the window, working on the theory that if she wasn't looking at him then he couldn't affect her. Hah! At this point she was beginning to think flying through a hurricane would have been easier on her nerves than this!

'Gee, Mum, you didn't have to get all dressed up!' Angie said, obviously surprised to see her mother make a public appearance in a T-shirt, biking shorts and runners.

Vanessa was equally quick to take in her daughter's appearance and happily decided that the girl looked extremely well. Craig, who was sitting on the edge of the bed holding his young wife's hand, looked only one breath away from being declared a corpse.

During the course of the next half-hour Angela revealed the details of the events leading up to her being hospitalised. Evidently Angela had complained to her obstetrician that she was passing water with abnormal regularity and that she thought she might have a chill in the kidneys as she was experiencing mild lower back discomfort. The doctor had immediately arranged for a series of urine tests and also requested that the baby be monitored for a short time. It was then that it was discovered Angie was in fact in labour—with contractions forty-five seconds apart!

'How could you not *know* that without a test?' Vanessa, whose first labour had been a horrendously long, painful experience, couldn't believe Angela hadn't recognised the symptoms.

'I've never had a baby before, have I? Besides, the doctor says some women have a very strong tolerance for pain,' Angela said proudly, obviously forgetting the time she'd hysterically demanded a general anaesthetic when she'd dislocated a finger playing netball and the doctor at the local casualty department had said that pulling it back into place was a simple matter.

Vanessa spent the next ten days travelling between the motel and the hospital, and trying to keep tabs on her business via long-distance phone calls. Angela's labour was being kept at bay with medication and the youngster was becoming increasingly bored by the limits the doctors placed on her walking. Vanessa found she was gritting her teeth to stop herself from telling her daughter she was acting like a selfish brat.

While she sympathised with the girl's frustration at not being allowed out of bed to do anything more than go to the bathroom, Vanessa felt that instead of complaining Angela should have been giving thanks for every day which bought her baby closer to full-term. Yet even a visit by Eleanor, cheerfully spouting all the possible horrors which could befall a premature baby, wasn't enough to halt Angela's appeals to the doctors to let her go home. That they caved in to her persistence was enough to whip Vanessa's temper to full-blown rage.

'Honestly, this is too, too ridiculous!' she fumed as an obviously overjoyed Angela emptied her bedside drawers and stuffed the contents into a large overnight bag. 'Where did these doctors get their degrees—the back of a cereal packet?'

'I don't care where they got them, I'm just glad I'm getting *out*!' Angie laughed and threw her arms around her husband.

'Me too,' he echoed, causing Vanessa to wheel around and glare at him.

'And how do you think you're going to feel when a doctor walks in and tells you that your child didn't make it?'

'Vanessa!' Mitch's voice rang from the door of the ward and, while Craig's face was ashen with fear, his was red with outrage.

'Mum, you've no right to say such things!' Angela burst

out. 'And, unlike some people, I'm not stupid enough to ride a horse!'

'That's enough, Angela!' The pain ripping through Vanessa would have sent her to the floor had it not been for Mitch's arm going around her waist. 'If I ever hear you say anything like that to your mother again...' she could feel the fury rumble through him '...I swear to God I'll beat you to within an inch of your life.' Craig's eyes said he'd have something to say about that, but Mitch cut him off before the words could leave his lips.

'Save it, O'Brien, we'll talk later. In the meantime, get Angie home and calmed down.'

Vanessa was too numb to do anything but allow Mitch to lead her from the ward and back to the hotel.

Zombie-like, she accepted the drink he mixed for her from the bar fridge in her room and made no objection when he then mixed another for himself.

'It's not going to do you any good if you don't drink it.'

She rubbed the back of her free hand across her eyes and groaned. 'It's not going to do me any good if I do.'

'It won't hurt.'

'No.' She looked across to where he sat in the room's only armchair. 'Not compared to the pain my daughter has just inflicted.'

Mitch studied his drink as if he were a scientist observing a mix of new chemicals.

'How much does she know, about...?'

'About *me killing our baby*?'

'*No!*' He leapt to his feet. 'Vanessa, don't say things like that! It was an *accident*. An unfortunate and tragic accident.'

She shook her head in despair rather than denial. 'You say that as if you mean it.'

'Of course I mean it! What the hell sort of comment is that to make?'

His handsome face was creased with confusion, disbelief

and pain, almost identical to that which she'd seen in it all those years ago, and it triggered her tears. Tears for a past she couldn't change, a present she couldn't control and a future shrouded by both.

The force of the sobs racking her body sent the drink she held slopping on to her feet, and she was only vaguely aware of the glass being removed from her fingers. She felt herself hauled against a stanchion of strength and the need for warmth and support urged her to hold firmly to it.

The tears burning her face drew their heat from the flames of her heartache. Heartache for the youthful passion and love lost to her past, for the child conceived in that love yet ultimately a victim to the passion. And for a grandchild of that love now hovering between safety and jeopardy.

Vanessa wasn't sure how long her tears lasted, but it was dark when she woke to find herself wrapped spoon-style in the arms of the man who knew her body better than any living soul. They were lying on top of the hotel bedspread, still full clothed. She smiled, realising that her uncontrolled crying jag could hardly have been expected to incite desire.

'Feeling better?' Mitch's voice was whisper-quiet at her ear.

'That depends on how you define "better".' With a fingernail she began tracing the intricate jacquard pattern of the bedspread. 'I know I owe Angela an apology. And Craig.'

'I think you owe them more than that.'

Vanessa's hand froze. 'Such as?'

'An explanation. How much does Angie know about what happened that day?'

Vanessa rolled away from him and got to her feet.

'Well?' he prompted.

'I...I don't know. I can hardly even remember her being there after...after...the fall.' She closed her eyes trying to force the painful images from her mind.

'Does she know what led up to you getting on the horse?' Mitch's voice held a hint of unsteadiness, but Vanessa refused to turn and see what was in his eyes. 'Does she fully understand why you left Brayburn and went to Perth?'

How could she, Vanessa thought, when even now she wasn't sure?

'Vanessa, talk to me,' Mitch urged. 'How much of what happened between us does Angie know about?'

'I…I don't know. I…' Vanessa paused in an effort to regain control of her trembling emotions. Damn him! Why did he have to keep dragging out the past when she was fighting to keep it at bay? Why couldn't he just let it rest; let their son rest?

'Did you ever tell her about the incident with me and Rachel?'

'Of course not!' She swung around, determined to put an end to his relentless line of questioning. 'Surely you don't think I'm that vindictive!'

Oh, lord, she wasn't up to this right now, she really wasn't!

'Look, Mitch, we aren't accomplishing anything by discussing this so let's drop the whole thing.'

'*Yet again.*'

She ignored him and began packing her clothes into her suitcase. The silence in the room was intense and she could feel Mitch's eye's following her every move. For several minutes she managed to hold her tongue, but eventually even a saint would have found it impossible.

'Must you watch every move I make? Surely you've seen a person pack before.'

'No,' he said. 'Remember, you left while I was out checking fences.'

Her hand froze on the snap of her suitcase. Didn't he ever give up? She refused to dignify the comment with a response and, after giving the bathroom a cursory check to see that she'd left nothing behind, she picked up her suitcase and looked pointedly at Mitch, still sprawled on the bed.

'Ready?' he questioned.

At her nod he rolled off the bed and pocketed his car keys from the side table before reaching for her luggage.

'Oh, by the way,' he said, and paused until she turned and looked at him. 'I'm going to tell both Angela and Craig my account of exactly what happened ten years ago. I'm not going to tolerate your being subjected to any more outbursts like today's, even out of ignorance.'

'Mitch, no.' Vanessa was touched by his concern, but also worried.

'Why? You're quite welcome to be present if you think I'll give an unfair account.'

'No, it's not that! Wait, please. Just until the baby's born. I don't want to frighten or upset Angie at a time like this.' She touched his hand. 'Please, Mitch, just wait a little longer?'

He closed eyes momentarily and sighed. 'Righto. If that's what you want.'

She nodded and smiled. 'Thank you.'

The urge to kiss his responding smile was strong; she almost succumbed to it, but suddenly the air was so sexually charged that she knew a solitary kiss, no matter how innocently given, was out of the question. She turned abruptly and practically ran to the door.

'You planning on staying at the main house or with Angela and Craig?' Mitch asked.

'With Angie, of course. She could go into labour at any time and someone's got to be with her when Craig's out working.'

Looking far from pleased, he jammed his Akubra on his head and stomped to the door, muttering under his breath.

Once back at Brayburn, however, Angie was even less receptive to the idea than her father had been.

'No way, Mum! There's only one bedroom and besides, I've just got married, I don't want my mother as a chaperon.'

'But Angie, you shouldn't be by yourself.'

'I won't be. At night Craig will be with me and during the day he can drop me up at the house before he starts work.'

'But that's so *early*. What if you want to sleep in?'

'Then I'll walk up later,' the teenager said logically as she strapped her seatbelt over her protruding stomach.

'You're not supposed to—'

'OK, OK! I'm not supposed to walk. Look, we can work out the details tomorrow; right now all I want to do is crawl into my own bed.'

Vanessa took her defeat in silence and watched as the darkness swallowed up the tail-lights of Craig's car.

'What about you?' Mitch asked from her side.

'Uh? What about me?' Her mind just couldn't function under the pressure of her overly active hormones.

'Are you determined to crawl into your own bed? Or could you be tempted by an alternative?'

'Mitch, I have no intention of sleeping with you, so get the idea right out of your head!'

Mitch grinned like a cheeky schoolboy.

'I don't know whose mind you *intended* reading, but the only thing on mine was a quiet drink.'

'No, thank you,' she said, trying to sound terse even as embarrassment rushed through her body like a raging flood. 'The last "quiet drink" we shared culminated in us waking up on the floor together naked!'

'Ah, now I see the connection! For a minute there I thought you must have been entertaining the idea of us sleeping together. My mistake.'

Seething over the fact that he knew he damned well hadn't made a mistake, Vanessa stormed into the house, slamming the door on his amused masculine chuckle.

This was just terrific! She was stuck out here sleeping under the same roof as the only man she'd ever loved, wanted or needed, and with her not to be trusted, totally unreliable hormones for possibly the next two months!

CHAPTER EIGHT

FOR days Vanessa was on constant guard and ready to deflect the slightest sexual advance or overtone Mitch made. The only trouble was, he didn't make any. Not one.

At first she was pleased he was prepared to abide by her rules, but gradually it began to annoy her. Did he have to make it seem so damned easy? It wasn't fair that he could be so totally immune to her, when one glance from him had her insides turning to mush and her heart pounding! And the risks she'd anticipated in entering a physical relationship with Mitch were becoming fewer and fewer in her mind.

The changes which had taken place in him over the years went way beyond the fine lines etched at the corners of his eyes and mouth. The Mitch Randall of today was less intense, less driven by the need to prove himself than the twenty-eight-year-old she'd left. He was more aware of, and more responsive to, the unspoken feelings of others. His single-minded need always to be in control seemed to have frayed a little at the edges, softened like aged denim.

But she'd changed too, in a vastly different way. Where Mitch had mellowed, she'd hardened, not simply because of the passing of time, but because it had been necessary. Because she'd had to stop herself from feeling like a victim, stop letting her life just happen and actually take some responsibility for it. With determination and hard work she'd done just that.

Vanessa knew she was now ready for a relationship in her

life; it was the final step in her emotional evolution. But was Mitch the right one to take that step with?

Oh, yes, she found the older Mitch very appealing and very, very exciting! But it worried her that perhaps Mitch hadn't learned to distinguish the Vanessa of ten years ago from the woman she was today. If a relationship between the two of them was to have any future, *both* she and Mitch had to accept the other for the person they had become rather than the person they had been. Could Mitch?

'Vanessa, are you listening?'

She looked up to meet Cora's frown and Mitch's faintly amused smile.

'Sorry?'

'Something wrong with your steak?' the housekeeper demanded.

'No, it's fine,' Vanessa said, knowing she'd made little impression on her meal.

'So how come you haven't finished it? You're not on some damn fool diet, are you?' Her tone was impatient. 'You're skinny enough now!'

'I'm not *skinny*, nor am I on a diet,' Vanessa countered, aware that Mitch was taking great delight in the byplay.

'So, you going to finish the steak or do you want me to take your plate?'

'I'll finish the steak,' Vanessa answered, obediently picking up her knife and fork.

'Oh, by the way, Cora,' Mitch said as the woman exchanged his empty dinner plate for a full dessert one, 'I'll be going out tomorrow night to a cattleman's dinner, so you'll only have to cook for Vanessa.'

'Huh!' grunted the older woman. 'Waste of electricity the amount she eats! Why don't you do the decent thing and take skinny minnie there with you and let me have a night off? Besides, it's a dinner dance, and I think she could use the R&R.'

Ordinarily Vanessa would have objected to being talked about as if she weren't there, but she found herself holding her breath for Mitch's response. A strained look came into his eyes and only someone who knew him well would have identified the slight uneasiness in his tone.

'I was planning on spending the night in town,' he said. 'It's a long drive, so it makes more sense to stay in town.'

It suddenly occurred to Vanessa that it was quite possible Mitch had a date! She bit down on a piece of prime beef and tasted only jealousy.

'Besides,' he added, 'I hardly think Vanessa would be interested in attending.'

'Why not? This place is half hers.' Cora turned her gaze directly on to Vanessa. 'Well?'

Mitch however gave her no time to respond.

'Nessa's never been interested in anything to do with the practical side of Brayburn; she's—'

'Now just one minute!' Jumping to her feet, Vanessa glared at him. 'That's not true! As a kid I was involved in everything from mustering to branding! And given a chance I could still do it with my eyes shut!'

'Vanessa, calm down,' he said.

'Look, I can't understand a word that's being said, so I might as well take myself off,' Cora announced in a loud voice, no doubt having gleaned from Vanessa's body language that the younger woman was shouting. 'I'll be in the kitchen if you need me.'

'Only if I want a hornet's nest stirred up!' Mitch muttered.

'She wasn't the one who stirred me up, Mitch,' Vanessa accused.

'She's the one who suggested I ask you to come tomorrow night.'

'But why say I wasn't interested in the cattle side of Brayburn? Why couldn't you just be honest and say you had a date?'

'What date?'

'The date you have tomorrow night.'

Mitch was frowning. 'I repeat...*what date?*'

'Oh, for God's sake, Mitch, stop being so totally immature! If you don't want to tell me the name of the woman you're staying in town with tomorrow night, that's fine.' A slow smile spread across his face and he rose from his chair. 'But at least be honest enough to admit there is one. It's not as if we're married any more. You don't have to protect me from the facts of life—'

'Thank God for that,' he groaned, hauling her into his arms. 'Because the last two weeks have just about killed me!'

His lips closed over hers before she could even think of the word 'struggle', and in less than a second the only ones she was capable of formulating were ones like 'bliss', 'magic' and 'heaven'. When the kiss finally ended, the only struggle was for air. Still they held each other.

'So,' Mitch said, running his fingers through her hair and making her tingle, 'would you care to accompany me to the cattleman's dinner tomorrow night?'

'You don't have a date?' she asked knowing from his eyes that he hadn't.

'Uh-uh, you're supposed to say, "You've got a date",' Mitch teased.

'OK. You've got a date, Mitch Randall.' It wasn't until she said the words that their meaning really registered. Her frown was a reflexive action.

'What's up?' Mitch queried, stroking her wrinkled brow with gentle fingers.

'Do you realise that we've never been on an actual date? Never in the twelve months that we knew each other before we got married did we date. *Really* date. We never even left the property! We became friends and then lovers, and then husband and wife, and then parents, without ever once going through the motions of dating!'

'Kinda weird when you think about it.'

'Weird? Bizarre is more like it. Ah!' Her squeal was a reaction to Mitch swinging her into his arms. 'What are you doing?'

'Saving you the effort of having to walk to the bedroom,' he grinned, striding to the door.

Vanessa couldn't decide whether it was Mitch's cavalier attitude or simply just his blind assumption that she *would* make love with him that put her hackles up, but she was definitely ticked off!

'Put me down.' Her command came out in a breathy whisper. OK, so maybe his assumption hadn't been totally visually impaired! But that wasn't the point.

'I mean it, Mitch,' she said more firmly. 'Put me down.'

His blue eyes held hers. 'Why?' he asked, the hand of his arm supporting her upper body brushing against her breast, causing tiny sparks which aroused her nipples.

She closed her eyes. 'Because.'

'Because—' he lowered his voice to a whisper and his mouth to her ear '—why?'

'Because...because...'

'Mmm?' he prompted, his lips now sliding down the column of her throat. Sensing that her control was only a smidgen away from collapse, she forced herself to focus on the table.

'You were saying...' Mitch's sexy smile almost undid her and she said the first thing that came into her head.

'I haven't finished my dinner.'

Instantly the kisses stopped and she found herself looking into an astonished male face.

'You're kidding! You want to eat? *Now*?'

Of course she didn't *want* to eat—well, not food at any rate! But she couldn't just fall back into bed yet again. Just because sex with Mitch was a banquet for her body, it didn't necessarily nourish her heart. Her feelings must have shown on her face, because Mitch quickly placed her on her feet and took several steps backwards.

'OK,' he said tersely. 'I'll concede you this round. But don't think I'll let you back out of tomorrow night.'

'Oh, I have no intention of backing out of our dinner date,' she told him.

The next morning Mitch entered the kitchen just as Vanessa was pouring her second cup of coffee. The million-megawatt smile he gave her caused her hand to tremble slightly.

'I thought since Cora's spending the morning with Angie you might like to ride out and check some of the cattle with me. You seemed pretty anxious for some hands-on involvement with them last night.'

Thrilled at the unexpected invitation, she hastily got to her feet.

'Of course, since you're not dressed for it,' Mitch said, frowning at her skirt and blouse, 'I could probably come up with some alternative *hands-on* activities right here. Course, you wouldn't be dressed for that either...'

She met his suggestive look with a smile. 'It won't take me a second to change. Have a coffee while you're waiting.'

'OK, but feel free to sing out if you need a hand getting anything off,' he said generously.

She laughed, sensing that, despite his provocative words, she and Mitch were embarking on a new relationship which had no ties with the past. She prayed she was right.

The temperature during the last week had consistently hovered between thirty-five and forty degrees Celsius and she suspected it exceeded that today. Her shirt was glued to her back and, regardless of how many times she wiped her brow on her sleeve, it was impossible to stop the beading of perspiration for more than a few minutes.

'You want to head back?' The brim of Mitch's hat shaded

his expression from view, but his concern was evident in his voice.

'I thought you said you still had to check out the cattle down near the bore?'

'I do. But there's no need for you to suffer this stinkin' heat any longer.'

'Of course there is,' she argued. 'I don't want you telling everyone at the dinner tonight that I wimped out on account of a little heat.'

'How about if I dress it up as complete and utter heat exhaustion?' he teased.

'No way. I can handle it.'

He didn't look totally convinced.

'Mitch, I'm fine. Really.'

'OK, but we'll head down to the creek and water the horses first.'

The particular section of the creek they went to was only about a metre deep, but it was shaded by a clump of majestic eucalyptus.

'I'd forgotten what a pretty spot this was,' Vanessa observed aloud as she stood holding her mount's reins while he drank. 'I used to come here a lot after Angie started school.'

'And do what?'

A sad laugh spilled from her lips. 'Nothing. There was never anything I could do—or so I was always being told.'

'By whom?'

She shrugged. 'If I listed everyone by name from the time I started boarding school, I'd never make that dinner tonight.'

'I prefer to think of it as our first date.'

She blushed. 'Sounds a bit silly calling it a date, when we're only a breath away from being grandparents.'

He took the reins from her hand and tied both horses to a low branch, before sitting down at the base of a silver gum. His easy, graceful movements never ceased to amaze her or stir her pulse.

'Come here.' He patted the ground beside him. 'And tell me what you would have liked to be doing when you used to come here and do nothing.'

Right now the only thing she wanted to do was fall into his arms, but she sensed Mitch really wanted to know. More importantly, she realised *she* wanted him to know.

Staying where she was, she focused on the exact spot where she'd once come to spend hour upon endless hour.

'Some days I used to sit here wishing I could paint so I could capture all the beauty and serenity that drew me here. Then I'd realise that I couldn't, because no one who felt so lonely and confused could hope to even come close to duplicating serenity.' She laughed. 'Of course, there was also the added problem which my former art mistress described as an imbalance between my appreciation and my co-ordination.'

'Meaning?'

'Meaning, I could recognise good art, but I couldn't paint for nuts!'

'What else did you think about doing?'

'I *thought* about doing lots of things. *Anything!*'

The bemused look on his face came as no real surprise to her. His accusations of the previous night had already shown how little he'd known about the girl he'd married. She looked at the sky wondering how to put into words what she'd felt at the time.

'Vanessa, you never *said* anything. I never realised.'

'I know.' She looked directly at him. 'You know, Mitch, if you'd done, back then, what you did this morning and asked me to check fences with you, I think it would have been a toss-up whether I'd have died of shock or elation. Then again, there were times when I wondered whether anyone would even know the difference if I did die.'

'Vanessa!'

'I'm not saying I contemplated *suicide*, Mitch, only that I had no sense of self-worth. If I'd walked out then instead of…'

'Why didn't you?'

'It was simply easier to stay. I had a five-year-old child and no qualifications. What was I going to do, besides fulfil my father's prophecy that I'd end up like my mother, flitting from one bad marriage to another simply for security?'

'Is that why you started studying again by correspondence? So you could eventually leave me?' His eyes were hurt.

'No.' Leaving him had never been something she'd chosen or decided to do. It had been an impulsive act of desperation— years later.

'I started doing correspondence courses because I was bored. You only seemed to need me in...in bed.' She swallowed quickly and hurried on. 'Angie was at school all day, and even the housekeeper told me that my biggest contribution to the domestic scene would be to stay out of it!'

'Why didn't you fire the bitch?' Mitch demanded, getting to his feet and coming towards her.

'It...it never occurred to me that I could. You insisted I needed one, so I assumed that meant you thought I was pretty much useless too.'

Less than two feet separated them. She continued speaking, wondering if he could hear her over the drumming of her pulse.

'I thought you liked her, Mitch. You never complained—'

'Nessa, I *hated* the old dragon! I only got her to make things easier for you. But,' he said, removing her hat, 'as you've pointed out, my communication skills were restricted to the bedroom and my brains were below my belt.' He lifted her chin and looked solemnly into her eyes. 'I'm sorry, Vanessa. So very, very sorry.'

His kiss was so achingly tender it brought tears to her eyes. When it ended far too quickly, she lifted her lashes and saw a look of adoration on Mitch's face.

His fingers combed her hair from the scalp to the ends, sending a shower of sparks down her spine. Then he transferred their attentions to her neck and throat and her head lolled back, her eyes closed, savouring the ecstasy in his touch. She clutched at his waist, afraid her legs would buckle, and immediately his arms were around her and holding her fast to his body.

'While I'll apologise for not understanding what you were going through back then,' he told her, 'I can't apologise for wanting you. *That* is congenital and—' he brushed his lips over hers '—incurable.'

His lips moved to her chin before trailing along her jaw, then cheekily his tongue flicked back and forth across her earlobe before moving on to her eyelid and then her brow. It was incredibly sensual and annoyingly frustrating!

'Ah, Mitch, just *kiss* me!' She almost moaned the words. She felt his amused chuckle in the vibration of his body and knew she was being ignored as his lips edged along her hairline. Mercifully the teasing ended a few seconds later. When it did, she shoved her hands into his hair to prevent any more evasiveness on the part of his lips.

The last clear thought she had as, locked together, they sank to the ground, was that maybe God was giving them a second chance.

A burring sound stunned them to stillness a short time later and with no more than a worried exchange of glances they hurried to their feet.

Mitch had been carrying the mobile phone everywhere with him ever since Angela had come home from the hospital so that he could be reached easily in an emergency. The doctors had been hoping to hold off Angela's labour for another three weeks at least and Vanessa's heart was in her mouth as she watched him extract it from the saddle-bag.

'What's up?' he demanded, and Vanessa felt fear gnaw at her as his face turned from worry to outright disappointment.

'What's the matter?' she asked, tugging at his arm. 'What's

happened? Is An—?' Her words died as he shrugged her away and continued speaking into the phone.

'Yeah, OK. We're on our way back, but in future don't bother to call me unless it's a life and death emergency,' he told the caller. 'You took fifty years off my life.'

'What's up?' Vanessa asked when it was obvious the call was finished. 'Is something wrong with Angie?'

'*That* was Angie. Seems your manager has been phoning all morning and sending faxes as if they were going out of style.'

The relief she'd felt on learning Angie was OK was quickly replaced by confusion. Not so much because of her staff's need to contact her, but by Mitch's obvious agitation.

'Mitch?'

He tucked his shirt into his pants without looking at her.

'Apparently some hotshot from Paris is arriving tomorrow and he wants to see you.'

'Oh, my God! Not Jacques du Pont?'

'Hell, Vanessa, it could be Jacques Cousteau for all I know!'

'I only asked! There's no need to snap my head off!'

'Sorry.' His apology sounded more automatic than sincere. 'Guess this means I'll be going stag to the dinner tonight, after all.'

Vanessa was suffering the effects of having been buffeted by too many different emotions in too short a space of time to be able to logically collate her thoughts into any sort of response. She watched in silence while he retrieved both their hats, then tossed hers at her, not caring that it landed at her feet.

'I've got to check those cattle up by the bore,' he said, looking anywhere but at her. 'Angie said Craig would drive you to the airport, but I'll be back at the house in a couple of hours and since I've got to go into town anyway I might as well save him the trip. I'll see you later.'

He heeled his mount into a canter and left her staring after him.

Vanessa dumped the entire contents of her underwear drawer willy-nilly into her suitcase, then swore when the lid refused to close.

She hated packing! She loathed and despised it! And she'd spent so much time doing it in the last three months, she'd have been qualified to teach courses in it! Of course it wasn't the actual packing she detested so much as the implications of it. Flying; boarding yet another vibrating, claustrophobic lump of metal hurtling lord knew how many kilometres above the earth, tempting heaven knew what disasters.

'Having trouble?' Cora asked from the bedroom doorway.

'No more than usual, but I'm finally ready. Is Mitch back yet?'

'He's taking a shower. I've just made a pot of tea; do you want to have a cup while you're waiting for him?'

'Thanks.' Vanessa smiled. 'I'll be down in a few minutes.'

'You look real nice,' the older woman complimented. 'Just like one of those women in a fashion magazine.'

'Ta, but just between you and me after wearing jeans for so long I feel overdressed!' Vanessa admitted, yet once Cora left she hurriedly caught her hair into a sleek top-knot and then spent several minutes deliberately trying to make it artfully untidy.

Before leaving the room she cast a final look in the mirror. Her make-up was professionally perfect and gave no indication of the problems she'd endured trying to get her eyeliner *just so*. The camel-coloured sheath dress she wore was in a Lycra-cotton mix ending about four inches above her knees, and showed her figure to advantage without looking tarty. Her low-heeled court shoes matched the dress so, to break the monotony of colour, she'd added a metallic black chain-belt, black hoop earrings and a large black watch.

She looked exactly as a successful businesswoman in the fashion field should. And lets face it, she was. The House of du Pont didn't consider just anybody to retail their garments. In the fashion world a personal visit from the heir to the company rated higher than an audience with the Pope. So why wasn't she jumping out of her skin with excitement? Why was she practically having to force herself to generate even a skerrick of enthusiasm for what lay ahead? Wasn't this what she'd dreamed of for four years? Worked obsessively towards for the last two?

Of course it was! And as little as four months ago this would have made her happier than anything else. But for the first time in ten years she was forced to acknowledge that career successes weren't going to be able to compensate for the failures in her personal life.

Turning from the mirror, she picked up her handbag and headed downstairs to the kitchen.

Angela and Craig were waiting to say goodbye and wish her luck, and Angie's parting words had been a promise not to go into labour until her mother's return.

'I'd love to have a written guarantee on that,' Vanessa told Cora. 'I just can't believe the incredibly bad timing of all this. Du Pont wasn't expected for months yet.'

'You can't defer the meeting?'

'Cora,' Vanessa said with emphasis, 'Jacques du Pont would never understand how anyone could let something as routine as childbirth stand in the way of a business deal.' She sighed. 'I hate leaving, even for a few days, with Angie's condition being so uncertain.'

'It's not leaving Angie that's worrying you. It's leaving her father.'

Vanessa opened her mouth to deny the accusation, but Cora didn't give her a chance.

'You're in love with Mitch and you can deny it till the sun

comes up in the west, but you're not going to convince neither yourself or me otherwise.'

'I don't lo—' Under the shrewd but kindly gaze of the housekeeper her intended denial died and she managed to produce an ironic smile. 'You don't miss much, do you, Cora?'

'I'm deaf, not stupid,' came the matter of fact response. 'And besides, Blind Freddy could see what was going on around here. A person can't be in the same room as you pair without feeling like they're walking into a tangle of live wires!'

'To me it seems more like a minefield,' Vanessa said sadly. 'No matter which way I step I'm going to end up being destroyed emotionally. Or at best maimed. If not me, then Mitch. We've been there, done that, Cora.' She shook her head. 'And that's why we're divorced.'

'Pah!' Cora dismissed the fact with a wave of her hand. 'Doesn't mean a thing! Being divorced doesn't stop a person from falling in love again. Happens all the time.'

'Yes, but not usually with the ex-spouse,' Vanessa said drily. 'Most people learn from their mistakes.'

'Or try to rectify them if they're given the chance.'

'Some things can't be rectified,' Vanessa said sadly. 'Some wounds go too deep.'

'Love's the greatest healer of all.'

'Even *unrequited* love?'

'I wasn't aware we were discussing unrequited love.'

'Has Mitch told you he loves me?' At the housekeeper's negative look she added, 'I didn't think so.'

'I can't hear with my ears, so I've learned to listen with my heart. The heart can hear what isn't said aloud,' Cora told her gently. 'But you're letting the screams of past pain deafen you to what your heart is hearing.'

Suddenly the façade she'd erected around her feelings crumbled. Tears welled in her eyes and her hand shook so badly she spilt her tea. Cora quickly removed the cup from her hand and replaced it with a tissue.

'Goodness, don't cry,' the woman admonished. 'It took you long enough to get yourself all made-up in the first place. You'll never make your flight if you have to start over.'

'But Cora—' tears were again dangerously close '—you've no idea how painful the past has been. Regardless of how I feel about Mitch now, I can't forget how much we've hurt each other.'

'The way I see it, it's not the *forgetting* of the past that's important, it's the *forgiving*. If you're waiting around for total amnesia to strike the pair of you so you can get on with the future,' she shrugged, 'then you're not going to have one.'

'Not going to have what?' Mitch entered the kitchen, still shower-fresh.

'Time for another cup of tea,' the housekeeper said smoothly, saving Vanessa the effort of having to formulate a sensible response in a clouded brain.

'I...I'll just go grab my luggage,' Vanessa said, rising from her chair.

'I've already put it in the car.'

'Oh, well. I guess I'm ready, then.' She kissed Cora on the cheek. 'Thank you for...for...the tea. I only wish you'd been here ten years ago.'

'The dinner dance is informal, huh?' Vanessa asked as Mitch climbed behind the wheel of the four wheel drive.

'Smart-casual,' he responded coolly without looking at her.

'You...look nice.' If that wasn't the understatement of all time!

A half-smile lightened his profile. 'For a bushie who doesn't own an imported sports coat.'

'In my opinion a Country Road design will hold its own against any casual label in the world.' But boy, could they quadruple their sales if they used Mitch as a model!

'How can you tell what brand this is just by looking?' he asked.

'Clothes are my business,' she said, telling herself to banish the illicit thoughts his nearness prompted and shoving on her sunglasses in case she couldn't and he read them in her eyes. 'Besides, most of the top names have a distinctive style which is recognisable.'

'So's yours. And I'm not just talking about the way you dress. Which incidentally today qualifies as a cross between chicly professional and sexy as sin!'

The appreciative gaze he sent her was slow and hot. It made her ache and blush all over. 'Th...thank you.' Her stammered reply was barely audible to her own ears.

'So this French bloke you've got to see...he's important, huh?'

She was so grateful for the switch of topic that she scarcely managed to stifle a relieved sigh.

'Yes. Jacques du Pont is the heir to one of the fastest growing fashion houses in the world. If I can convince him I'm the right person to handle the sale of du Pont creations in Australia it'll be the fashion coup of the year.'

'I'm impressed.'

'Let's hope Monsieur de Pont is too.'

'When are you supposed to meet him? Tonight?'

'No, not until tomorrow. Thank God!' she added. 'Tonight I'm going to be flat out briefing my staff.'

'Despite the last-minute rush, you're excited by this.' Mitch sent her a knowing smile. 'I can hear it in your voice.'

She half suspected that the excitement in her was created as much by him as anything else, but she wasn't about to say so.

'It's one of the things I've dreamed of for a long time. So, yeah, I guess I'm excited.' She gave a rueful smile. 'But I'm also very nervous.'

The touch of his hand grasping hers was so unexpected it

stalled her lungs, but the ensuing squeeze to her fingers kick-started them back into action and the end result was a half-strangled gasp.

'Relax,' he said, blue eyes alight with tenderness. 'You'll do fine, Nessa. Just fine.' He returned his gaze to the road and his hand to the steering-wheel. 'Try thinking about something else for a while.'

Good advice, she was sure, but since the only other subject capable of occupying her thoughts for more than two seconds was Mitch himself, worrying about du Pont seemed to be erring on the side of caution. She rested her head back against the seat and gazed out of the window, trying desperately to concentrate on what she had to do tomorrow. Beside her, God's gift to women started to whistle along with the radio...

The sight of the airport turned her stomach into a flight path for supersonic jets.

Relax, you can handle it. Relax, you can handle it. Relax, you can handle it.

The silent chant was one she practised religiously every time she was about to set foot on a plane. Once on the aircraft it was superseded by a non-stop recital of the Lord's Prayer, right up until she'd safely disembarked at her destination.

'Vanessa?' At the sound of Mitch's voice she opened her eyes. 'We're here,' he said, the concerned look on his face making her realise that she no doubt looked like an idiot.

She made a conscious effort to uncurl her fingers from their death grip on her handbag and forced a smile as she unsnapped her seatbelt.

'Flying really does scare you, doesn't it?'

'I've never made a secret of the fact.'

'I know, but I've never seen you only moments before you've boarded.'

'Be grateful. Some airline stewards have been known to quit their jobs at the sight of my name on a passenger list.'

He grinned. 'At least you can joke about it.'

'Who's joking?' she responded as she got out of the car. 'You think the Pope's the only person who gets out of a plane and kisses the ground?'

He shook his head in amusement and opened the vehicle's rear door to take out the luggage. Vanessa knew she should have put her own bags in the car as soon as she sighted the battered black suitcase Mitch pulled out.

'Oh, God, no!' she wailed. 'You've made a mistake!'

'No mistake.'

'Dammit, Mitch, I know what luggage I packed!' Vanessa shouted. *That isn't my bag!*'

'Nope, this is my bag,' he said calmly. 'And these two,' he groaned, 'which have obviously been weighted down with bricks, are yours.'

'Sorry, I…I forgot you said you were staying in town to-night,' she muttered, feeling every kind of a fool. 'It's just I'm so strung out about tomorrow and flying and…and everything, that I'm expecting something to go wrong. Forgetting my suit-cases was only one of the scenarios I imagined.'

'Nothing's going to go wrong.'

'That's easy for you to say.' She frowned as Mitch struggled to pick up all three cases. 'Wouldn't it make more sense to leave your bag in the car?'

'Not really. What'll I do for clothes once we get to Perth?'

As Vanessa staggered backwards in shock, Mitch sent her devastating smile.

'I did warn you that I wasn't going to let you back out of our dinner date…'

CHAPTER NINE

'Now I know how a sardine feels,' Mitch complained as he tried to make his six-foot frame comfortable in the limited area allotted to passengers on the small Fokker Friendship. 'How come you don't fly business class, where they advertise extra leg-room?'

'There's no such thing as business class on a plane this size. And even if there were, I wouldn't travel in it.'

'Why not?'

'Because I like to sit right over the wings, next to the doors.'

Vanessa might well have still been numb over Mitch's uncharacteristically impulsive decision to accompany her clear across the country on nothing more than a couple of hours' notice, but not so numb that she didn't notice the second the plane started to taxi down the run.

'Dear God,' she muttered. 'Please let us make the connecting flight in Sydney in one piece.'

'You aren't worried about the second stage of the trip to Perth?' Mitch's voice was tinged with amusement, but Vanessa didn't bother opening her eyes to see if he was smiling.

'I take it bit by bit.'

'Don't want to ask for too much in one go, huh?'

'Don't want to think that far ahead.' The plane started to lift. 'Oh, hell.'

Mitch chuckled. 'From heaven to hell in a matter of seconds. You sure do get around.'

'Mitch,' she hissed, her eyes still closed. 'Will you shut up? I can't concentrate.'

'What are you trying to "concentrate" on?'

'On keeping this stupid plane in the air!'

His laughter was like an explosion in the confined space. Vanessa's eyes opened to glare at him, only to find they were drawing attention from nearby passengers.

'You're concentrating on keeping the plane up?' Amusement was making his eyes tear. 'You want me to go tell the pilot so he can take a break? No point you both wearing yourselves out mentally this trip.'

'*Will you shut up*? Everyone is staring at us.'

'I'm only trying to take your mind off things.'

'Well, don't! OK?' Vanessa hated people knowing how frightened she was and she preferred to deal with the fear in her own way. 'I can handle this.'

Despite this assertion, she didn't withdraw her hand when Mitch closed his own over it, and she couldn't swear that her rapid heart-rate was solely the result of her phobia.

The flight from Tamworth to Sydney was quick and surprisingly smooth; apart from the usual paralysis which attacked her during the landing descent, Vanessa considered she'd coped well. But as soon as they were seated on the connecting flight to Perth fear again consumed her body and she fell into her usual method of trying to deal with it. After a few minutes Mitch intruded on the spiritual litany.

'Nessa. Nessa!' he whispered urgently. 'You know what?'

'What?' she echoed, turning towards him.

His hand captured her chin to stop her turning away, but it wasn't necessary since the look in his eyes was enough to immobilise her. 'You're beautiful.'

Her lips needed no persuasion to open beneath his kiss. It would have been easier for her to accept sitting on the wing all the way to Perth than to deny herself the taste of the man she loved. As kisses went it seemed to run the gamut of emotions from wholesomely sweet to erotically passionate, but at every stage it ignited feelings in her that had only and would only ever be aroused by this man.

When they finally parted he appeared as stunned as she felt.

'Wow,' he said. 'I wonder if we should credit that to the altitude?'

'We haven't lifted off yet.'

'Any closer,' he muttered, shifting awkwardly in his seat to mask the fact that his trousers were suddenly too tight, 'and I'll risk being arrested.'

Vanessa couldn't help smiling at the craziness of the situation.

'Mitch, are you trying to draw attention to us again?'

'Nope, I'm trying to distract you again,' he said with a wink. 'Is it working?'

Oh, God, it was working all right!

Although there were several occasions when the plane encountered pockets of rough air which instantly turned Vanessa rigid with terror, being with Mitch did make the flying less of an ordeal than usual.

They'd discussed Mitch's plans for Brayburn for the next couple of years, and his announcement that his brother Cam had convinced him to try his hand at thoroughbred breeding pleased Vanessa. Though on reflection she'd probably have been better advised to curb her enthusiasm for the idea a little, since it had caused Mitch to ask if it meant she was ready to take a more active interest in the property.

She managed to sidestep giving a direct answer by pointing out how much busier she would be if she was lucky enough to cut a deal with Jacques du Pont. Mitch then became obsessed with knowing practically everything there was to know about her business, right down to the qualifications of her staff!

Now, as she looked across at the solid male figure beside her, his eyes were closed and his face restful. Beneath the cotton of his shirt his chest rose and fell in a hypnotic, even rhythm. She wished she felt half as relaxed as he looked, but the emotions churning through her couldn't be curbed by mere wishful thinking.

They were fifteen minutes away from landing, but the rapid palpitations of her heart could only partly be attributed to that. She hadn't been able to verbalise her questions regarding Mitch's decision to escort her to Perth. She wasn't so stupid that she didn't recognise it as an obvious statement that he wanted to be with her, but she wanted to know where he expected such an orchestrated display of impulsiveness would leave them. It would help if at least one of them had some idea!

Did he see this trip as an opportunity for a quick fling or as a springboard for something more? Did he expect she would relegate her business affairs to second place behind him? Or was this some sort of test? If so, a test for whom?

Their relationship had never ventured beyond the perimeters of Brayburn. It had been born there, thrived for a time, then wilted and finally died there. For years she believed that, like Samuel, it too had been buried there. Now she felt otherwise. Yet could this born-again, almost embryonic love survive being prematurely thrust into a world which could only emphasise to Mitch how much she'd changed?

His hand caressed the side of her neck, sending a tremor of awareness through her.

'Are you sure about this, Nessa?' he asked, not taking his eyes from hers. 'I could stay at a hotel.'

'I'm sure, about you staying here,' she said. 'Beyond that I'm not sure of anything.' She turned away and put almost the width of the lounge between them.

Looking around at the modern black and white décor, she

wondered if Mitch realised how much his presence seemed to jar with the room. He didn't belong amid the glass and chrome furnishings. Even dressed in a sports coat and trousers there was a raw quality about him that overpowered the smooth, polished trappings of urban normality, and yet Vanessa knew when he left his aura would be indelibly stamped into the apartment's atmosphere.

She felt his approach even before he took her shoulders and drew her back against him. Strangely, his touch drained much of the tension from her, and as she sagged into his strength her body felt his sigh.

'Why are you here, Mitch?' she asked. It was several moments before she got any response.

'I'm not sure,' he said finally. 'All I know is, I couldn't stand the thought of wondering when you'd be coming back.'

The touch of his tongue against her neck electrified her, its slick wetness produced a similar feeling lower in her anatomy. Her groan was echoed by one of Mitch's.

'I told you'd I'd only have to be here a few days,' she said, trying to ignore the liquid heat consuming her. 'I said a...a week tops.' Her head tilted to afford him more access to her.

'It's the waiting that's the killer.'

As he muttered the moist words his arms came around her hips and his palms slid down over her thighs. Slowly he began hitching her dress up centimetre by centimetre. A sensual shiver slithered down her spine and passion was dissolving her skin.

'Ah, Nessa, honey. You feel so bloody good. Forget whatever you have to do and just stay here. I want to love you until neither of us can breathe.'

His words triggered a pain in her heart. It was an old pain, but that didn't make its current impact any less crippling. Calling on what minuscule resistance she still had, she freed herself from his embrace.

'I...can't,' she said, straightening first her clothes and then her stance, and looked into his desire-flushed face. 'I have things to sort out at the boutique. This du Pont deal is very important to me.'

'More important than us?' he challenged. 'Don't you think our relationship needs to be sorted out first?'

'You're incredible! You know that? Incredibly *self-centred* and incredibly *hypocritical*!'

'What's that supposed to mean?' he demanded.

'Only that it's a pity you didn't give *our relationship* top priority when we were married!' Vanessa accused. 'Or is its importance solely dependent on whether it interferes with your career?'

Mitch somehow managed to look totally perplexed by what she was saying and it only made her angrier.

'How can you expect me to do what you never did and then accuse me of having warped priorities?'

'Right now I'm beginning to think the only thing warped is this conversation!' he complained, running a hand through his thick curls. 'You want to run this last bit, the part about me not doing what I expect you to do, by me again? I'll settle for a concise abridged version this time,' he added drily.

'OK!' she agreed as if taking up a challenge. 'The bottom line is, you always put Brayburn ahead of me and our relationship! I lost count of the number of times I heard, "Listen, honey, this'll have to wait, I've got steers to brand," or "Vanessa, I don't have time for this, you decide!"'

'So this is pay-back time, uh? This is your way of getting even, is it?'

'Of course not! I...I...I simply want you to understand, that I've changed,' she said eventually. She watched his eyes so she could gauge his reaction to what she was saying. 'I'm not the same person I used to be. I agree we have to work out our...affa...er...our relationship or whatever it is that's happening between us!' He grinned as she grappled to find a suitable definition. 'Oh, you know what I mean!'

'Go on,' he prompted, shoving his hands into his pockets as if he had nothing better to do but listen.

'I've got commitments to a life beyond Brayburn now. I can't afford to let it slide just to satisfy my hormones. You of all people should understand that.'

'Yeah. I guess.' Mitch's mouth twisted in irony. 'I don't suppose you'd consider letting it slide for an hour or so just to satisfy *my* hormones?' he asked in a hopeful tone.

He looked so adorably sexy that Vanessa had to close her eyes to find the strength to shake her head.

'Sorry,' she smiled.

'Any chance of a rain-check?'

Her pulse was racing at the seductive timbre of his voice. She hedged, 'I'm going to be pretty flat-out the next couple of days.'

'Lady, if I had my way you'd be flat-out right now!'

She swallowed hard. 'I don't think prospective grandfathers are supposed to say things like that.'

'I don't think prospective grandmothers should wear sexy underwear,' he countered. 'So I'll be doing my damnedest to get you out of it.'

Vanessa left the room, barely able to breathe.

By the time she arrived at the boutique it was closed to the public so the staff were available to devote themselves entirely to carrying out Vanessa's instructions regarding Jacques du Pont's visit. Each of them recognised the importance of impressing the Frenchman and tension and excitement were thick in the air.

'Gee, you're positively glowing.'

At the sound of her manager's voice, Vanessa looked up. 'Perspiration will do that,' she responded, setting aside the details of her proposal to du Pont which she was reading yet again. 'This du Pont deal has really got me edgy.' She looked at the two cups of coffee the younger woman carried. 'I hope one of those is for me.'

'Of course. Never let it be said that Louisa Duncan doesn't know how to suck up to authority.'

'Good. Your job is safe.'

'For how long?'

The sudden seriousness in the woman's voice startled Vanessa. 'Pardon?'

'I want to know if you have plans to sell Standing Alone.' Direct brown eyes met Vanessa's.

'Where on earth would you get an idea like that?'

'It's not only me. The sales staff are speculating too. It's to be expected, Vanessa,' she said. 'You've spent more time away in the last few months than you have in the four years I've worked here.'

'That doesn't mean I intend to sell the business,' Vanessa stated. 'You know the circumstances with Angie. As a mother I didn't have a whole lot of choice.' Her manager nodded. 'So, what bought this on?'

'When I spoke to Angie the other day on the phone she said she didn't think you'd be thrilled at the idea of having to come racing back over here again. And it didn't sound like you were ODing on enthusiasm when I talked to you later.'

She hadn't been. And apparently it hadn't been a secret.

'I thought perhaps you were entertaining ideas of staying in the east and being a full-time granny.'

'*Granny*! I haven't decided on a title yet, but rest assured it won't be Granny!'

Lou laughed. 'I guess that reaction means you're still not thrilled at the prospect of joining the ranks of the lawn bowls crowd.'

'I'm coming to terms with sliding back one generation, but lawn bowls is definitely out. So,' she said firmly, 'is selling my business.'

The younger woman smiled her relief. 'Great. I really enjoy having you for a boss.'

'You're right,' Vanessa said. 'Your *sucking up* is second to none!'

When Lou left Vanessa didn't immediately return to the task she'd been doing before the interruption; instead she cradled her coffee-cup in both hands and contemplated its dark liquid contents.

No one understood that selling her store was something she'd never do. Not because she was obsessed with the idea of owning it, but because to her it was symbolic. It was representative of her independence and her ability to survive on her own...even now when she knew she no longer wanted to be alone. To sell it and move east would be not so much a case of putting all her eggs into a basket labelled 'Hope' as it would a retrograde step. And moving backwards might mean running the risk that she could again underscore her self worth.

She raised the cup to her lips and the cold bitterness of its contents alerted her to the fact she was wasting time. It was already after nine, but refusing to admit how tired she was she turned a yawn into a sigh and reached for the file marked du Pont.

It was ten past eleven when Vanessa slipped her key into the lock of her front door. Flickering light and the sound of an irreverent late-night talk show host gave her a clue to the fact that Mitch was still up. She dumped her attaché case on the hall stand then paused to ask herself if in fact she was glad he'd not gone to sleep.

The moment he appeared in her line of vision her heart gave her the answer.

'Hi,' she said, her voice sounding stupidly shy.

'Lord, Vanessa, you look absolutely bushed.'

While you, she thought, taking in his bare muscular torso and unruly damp curls, look absolutely gorgeous. He'd been crowding her thoughts even as she ploughed her way through the myriad things that needed to be co-ordinated for the meeting tomorrow. She would never have thought to ask him to accompany her on this trip to Perth, but having him here at the end of a trying day was wonderful. It made her life seem complete. It made *her* feel complete.

'You owe me a dinner date,' he reminded her. 'Are you hungry?'

She shook her head. 'Not for food.'

The smile he sent her was one that said he shared her sentiment.

He began walking down the hall and with each barefoot step he took Vanessa felt the heat rising in her. He stopped in front of her and cupped her face in his hands to gently stroke her cheekbones.

'You know something,' he said. 'You've been gone less than six hours and I've missed you more than I did in the ten years we were apart.'

The sad sincerity on his face tore at her heart and stung her eyes as the shower-fresh maleness of him invaded her nostrils. She inhaled deeply, not because she needed oxygen, but because his nearness was making her dizzy in ways which made her feel wonderful. In the seconds it took for him to lower his head to hers she imagined she could perhaps understand how an addict might feel snorting cocaine, but such analogies were forgotten as his mouth brushed hers.

Starved for the feel of him, her arms wrapped around his midriff, her soul quietly melting as his teeth nipped at her lower lip. Nothing would ever compare to the love she had for this man, and though she knew in her heart that there had never really been a time when she had stopped loving him, she'd *never* loved him like this!

She was conscious of his hands moving to her hips and the pressure of his tongue as it sought deeper entry. *Deeper entry!* A whimper escaped from her throat as a sensual fire roared through her body. Oh, yes, that was what she wanted. What she needed! Total and absolute absorption of this man. Mentally, physically and spiritually. Every way, forever. All ways and for always.

The need for air forced their mouths apart, so she compensated with the tip of her tongue in the absence of his by sliding it across his collarbone. His groan only inspired her nails to move from his waist to the furred hardness of his chest.

'Ah, Nessa…I thought…you…said…you…' the gaps in his speech were caused by his tongue swirling about the shell of her ear '…were…tired.' He eased back a fraction and lifted her face. 'Are you sure you're up to this?'

His consideration might have amused her if it weren't so misplaced. She slipped her hand to the hardness at the front of his jeans and smiled as his eyes shut on a groan of pure pleasure.

'I am tired, Mitch,' she confirmed solemnly. 'But the only way I'll be too tired to finish this is if my pulse stops.'

With a smile that promised salvation through sin he laid his hand over her left breast. 'Feels fine to me, if a tad erratic.'

Grinning, she unzipped his jeans and laid her hand over him.

'I'd say yours feels a tad…*erotic*.'

They never even made it as far as the bedroom… At least not on that occasion.

The last thing Vanessa felt like doing was untangling herself from the masculine arms and legs still wrapped around her and getting dressed for work. But today was the biggest day in her business life and she had to do exactly that. Sighing, she lifted her left leg and then freed her right by gently moving the male one pinning it to the mattress.

Only fierce determination stopped her from running her fingers up the said male leg until they could teasingly provoke the owner from sleep. Then, when her lower body was no longer held captive by the warm weight of the naked male at her side, she carefully untangled his hand from her hair and edged herself off the mattress.

Walking nude to the bathroom she caught sight of the randomly scattered clothes littering the hall. The memory of what had happened since her arrival home last night sent such a charge of desire through her she practically sprinted to the bathroom, fearing her resolve would weaken and she'd end up back in bed. She locked the door, then laughed at her own stupidity.

She was seriously contemplating the advantages of having a cold shower when she heard Mitch shouting for her.

'I'm in the bathroom,' she called back.

Within seconds the door-handle rattled. Locking it had been a smart move after all, she thought with a grin.

'Nessa, are you OK?'

'Sure. I'm taking a shower.'

'At this hour? It's…only twenty past five.'

'I know. Go back to bed. One of us might as well get some sleep.'

'I'd rather have a shower. Unlock the door.'

'No way. I'd never get to work.'

'You've got hours yet. C'mon, hon, open the door and I'll rub your back.' His cajoling tone made her smile.

'Said the spider to the fly!' she retorted turning on the water. 'Sorry, Mitch, but I've got to get ready for work.'

'Vanessa, you've got ages until—'

'No, I don't. I need to be at work by six-thirty.'

She stepped under the jet of water, drowning out the male voice on the other side of the door.

Five minutes later when she ventured into the kitchen Mitch was dressed and making coffee, but the smile which emerged at his presence froze the instant he turned to face her.

Automatically she clutched the front of her towelling robe,

not from any delayed sense of modesty, but simply because
the atmosphere in the room felt colder than ice.

'Mitch, what's the matter? What have I done?' A few weeks
ago such a look would have prompted her to assume that
something had happened to Angie or the baby. But instinctively she knew she'd personally provoked this.

'You honestly don't know, do you?' His eyes were nar-
rowed and stormy. 'You have no flamin' idea at all!' He
thumped the sink, then swore and raked his fingers through
his hair. 'Jeez, Vanessa, didn't last night mean anything to
you?'

'Of course it did! Ho...how could you think otherwise?'

'Hell, Vanessa, I don't know,' he said mockingly. 'Maybe
it's the fact that you're in such an all-fired hurry to just pretend
it didn't happen!'

Vanessa didn't know if she was more shocked than angered
by his accusation or vice versa.

'Even if you didn't think you could bluff your way through
a *deep and meaningful* this morning, the least you could have
done was woken me and said, "Thanks, it was fun!" Instead
of simply trying to sneak off to work as if it never happened!'

'I wasn't trying to sneak off to work!' Her denial was delivered through tear-misted eyes. 'I just didn't want to disturb
you. I knew you'd be tired after the plane trip and...and...it
was after three before we got to...sleep.'

'Don't tell me what time it was! I was there, remember!
But hell, lady, you've gotta be a whole lot more tired than I
am, 'cause your *performance* came right on the heels of not
only a transcontinental flight, but six hours of business!'

Vanessa winced at his tone and tried to concentrate on
squeezing the fabric of her robe to keep her tears at bay.

'If you can function on two hours' sleep, why assume I
can't?' he snapped.

'Damn it, Mitch! What is your problem? I—' She stopped

dead as the kitchen clock-radio automatically came on and the pips for the six o'clock news blasted into the air!

'Oh, no! I'm going to be late for work!'

Mitch swore violently and instantly had her attention again.

'Look, Mitch, I'm sorry I didn't wake you. But you're wrong, truly you are. Last night meant *everything* to me! It—' She had so much she wanted to say, but not now. Not like this. There wasn't time. 'But…oh, look, I have to get dressed or I'll be late. Today's important to me.'

'More important than it was yesterday? Or just more important than last night?'

'No! More important than it was yesterday *because* of last night.'

'Why?'

'Because…I… Oh, Mitch, I can't explain now. We can talk tonight. Please say you understand.'

Without a word he walked past her.

'Mitch, Mitch! Where are you—?' As the front door slammed on her words, she gave up the fight against tears, but not her fight to at least try and convince him of what he meant to her. She raced to the door and flung it open.

'Mitch! Mitch, I love you!'

The stairwell was deserted…

Vanessa had never felt so tired or utterly miserable. She slammed the door of her car then noticed she'd left her attaché case on the passenger seat along with her shoes.

'You are so stupid, Vanessa! Stupid, stupid, stupid!' Still holding the keys in her hand, she thumped the roof of the car once with her fist then lowered her forehead against the gleaming gunmetal-grey enamel and surrendered to the heartbreak she'd managed to keep at bay all day.

Forgetting the business side of things, her day had been a disaster. In fact her whole bloody life had been a disaster! She could keep telling herself from now till doomsday that she was a successful, independent woman, but that didn't make it so! Positive thinking, visualisation and every other stupid phrase psychoanalysts, social workers and all round do-gooders preached ad nauseam didn't mean diddly!

Love was the only vital ingredient to happiness. Good, solid, dependable two-way love! If a woman had that she had everything. If she didn't, Vanessa mused on a sniffle, well, then she probably stood in dimly lit garages, crying all over the paintwork of her car.

She let loose with a string of swear-words she hadn't used since she'd been a kid on Brayburn and stood up straight, wincing as the muscles in her neck objected.

'Damn you, Mitch Randall, wasn't a broken heart enough?' she muttered, massaging the knotted muscles. Deciding not to bother with her case and shoes, she walked from the garage in stockinged feet and, using the remote device on her keys, locked the door.

The building's car park was typically deserted; most of the residents were young, successful professionals who because of business or social commitments were rarely home before ten on week nights. Unable to control the flicker of irrational hope still gnawing at her, Vanessa lifted her eyes to the windows of her apartment. The absence of light brutally stabbed life from the final sliver of optimism which had clung to her heart.

A fresh tide of tears trickled down her face. At least, she thought they were fresh; she wasn't sure if she'd actually stopped crying at any point since leaving the boutique. She wasn't certain she ever would.

The search for the key which would open the security door rammed home the cruel hard fact that all her phone calls to the apartment that day had been an exercise in futility. Mitch couldn't have returned even if he wanted to, so the frantic pleas she'd left for him on her answering machine would be heard by no one but herself.

Inside the main door, she stopped and gazed forlornly up the staircase. Like this morning, it was empty.

Slowly she forced one foot in front of the other and climbed the stairs. Halfway up it occurred to her that if she could leave messages on her answering machine, so could Mitch!

She took the remaining stairs two at a time, swore like a sailor when she fumbled first with her keys and then with the door-handle, and finally flew into her unit like a tornado, flicking on the light as she went.

The call counter on her multipurpose phone was flashing the number twenty-three.

'Oh, please God,' she prayed as she flicked the play switch. 'Let me hear my voice only twenty-two times.'

It turned out she'd called only seventeen times. Susan had called twice, Angie three times—just to find out how the du Pont deal had gone—even her *mother* had called!

Everyone, bar the person she loved most of all.

CHAPTER TEN

SHE'D have probably stayed on her knees sobbing all night if the hammering at her door hadn't finally become too much to ignore.

'Damn it,' she said as she reefed open the front door. 'I told you to *go aw*—'

Her words stalled when she realised no one was there. Terrific! Not only was her heart shot to ribbons; her mind was going as well! No. She *could* hear hammering! Even now! Quickly she slammed the door and raced over to the sliding glass ones which opened on to the balcony overlooking the car park.

Nothing. She turned and hurried down the hall to her bedroom, aware not only that the closer she got to it the louder the banging became, but that someone was calling her name. No, not someone, *Mitch*! No one but Mitch ever called her Nessa.

'Mitch! Mitch, where are you?'

'Out here on the balcony.'

She flew to the huge double glass doors and tugged furiously to open the vertical blinds.

There he was; standing with his palms pressed against the glass, dressed as he'd been that morning, in a T-shirt, faded jeans and barefoot.

Her heart turned over and she didn't know whether to laugh or cry, and finally managed a half-strangled gasp of, 'Oh, Mitch...Mitch.'

Gently she pressed her hands against the glass, placing them directly opposite his and stared into the clear sky-blue of eyes.

'Nessa, I'm sorry,' he said, the anguish in his voice visible too in his handsome face. 'I acted like a bloody horse's rear.'

'Me too. I've been trying to call you all day.'

'I know. I've been out here since about three and the phone never stopped.' He frowned and lifted a finger to where her forehead rested against the glass. 'You've been crying...'

'I...thought I'd never see you again.' Her voice was a broken whisper, reflecting the pain such a notion had caused her.

'Did you forget we've still got to face at least *one* grand-child's christening?' His half-smile was endearingly sweet. 'I know you have every right to be annoyed, but surely you're not so cold-hearted you'd leave me to face the dreaded Eleanor on my own?'

She tried to smile, but wasn't sure it worked. 'Oh, Mitch...' She shook her head, trying to loosen the words she needed so desperately to say. 'There's so much I want to explain to you. And so much I want to ask you...' She sent him a helpless look. 'I don't know where to start.'

'I do.' He was watching her with infinite tenderness. 'Did you mean what you said this morning?' he asked hopefully.

She frowned.

'About loving me.'

'You...you *heard*!'

He nodded and stepped back from the glass. 'What I need to hear *now* is that you meant it.' His blue eyes held hers. 'Did you?'

She nodded wildly. '*Of course I meant it*! You idiot! I love you so much it hurts!'

He moved back to the glass, grinning. 'You're sure about this? I mean, you're not going to turn around in ten or twenty years' time and say you got it wrong, that what you feel is only passion or lust or a bad dose of flu or something?'

'No,' she said, knowing that her love would endure beyond the grave. 'I've quit lying to myself.'

'Good. 'Cos I want you to know I *never* stopped loving you. There hasn't been a day since I was eighteen years old that I haven't woken up wanting you and loving you.'

'Oh, Mitch...'

His words, his tone and the love emanating from his face was filling her with so much confidence for their future that it was making her tremble, and she had to try and talk around a huge lump in her throat.

'I want you too. So much...so very, very much.'

'Enough to open this door?'

'Wha— Oh!' She burst out laughing. 'Why didn't you remind me earlier?'

'Honey, I was getting so hot out here, I reckoned I'd be able to melt it eventually.'

'You're crazy,' she said, searching the top of her dressing-table for the key. 'You could have been killed climbing up there.'

'No way,' he said, his hand sliding the door open the moment the lock clicked. 'I've got too much to live for!'

Within seconds he'd pulled her into his arms and was squeezing her as if he'd never let her go. Vanessa prayed not as she returned his feverish hug with unabashed joy, kissing his neck, his throat, his ear, anywhere where the warmth of his flesh wasn't hidden behind fabric. Finally they paused to wordlessly search each other's faces. Then simultaneously their heads moved together.

Mitch's kiss started out as sedating, soft; little more than a series of passes across her slightly parted mouth. Then it escalated into an intoxicatingly sensual exploration of the tip of her tongue and the sleek enamel of her teeth. She clung to him, eagerly returning his oral affections as his hands roamed her body, setting her skin ablaze with just the slightest touch.

'Ah, Nessa. My beautiful, beautiful Nessa. I love you so

much,' he muttered, raining feverish butterfly kisses over her face. 'I swear I'll never hurt you again. Never, never again.' His hands went to the sides of her head and he held her face towards his. 'Promise me, *promise* me,' he begged, 'you'll never leave me again.'

His need to hear the words was like a visible pain in the blue depths of his eyes and the clenched hardness of his jaw. Yet underlying it was the startlingly clear image of his love.

Vanessa stroked a finger down his unshaven cheek and across the hard roughness of his jaw, before softly caressing first one cheekbone, then the other. She knew they had to dispel the past pain and fears totally, to bring their new love into the foreground. She raised her face to him, praying that everything he meant to her was displayed right there for him to see.

'I could never leave you, Mitch. I know now that I can't live without you.' He made a movement of disagreement, but she covered his mouth with her fingers before he could voice it.

'I don't mean I couldn't survive or exist without you,' she said. 'But I can't *live* without you. Not here,' she touched her heart. 'Not where it counts.'

'Nessa—'

'No, please.' She again covered his mouth. 'Let me finish. I love you, Mitch. I suppose I always have. But not like this. Not as a woman who doesn't *have* to depend on you, but who *wants* and *chooses* to depend on you.'

A smile spreading across his face distracted her.

'You're doing it again,' he grinned.

'Doing what?'

'Rationalising, analysing and—'

'If you say bullsh—'

'I wasn't going to,' he said. 'Just give me the concise abridged version.'

'I love you, Mitch Randall, with every ounce of passion in my body.'

'Can I have a demonstration of how much?' he asked, lifting her into his arms.

She smiled and linked her arms around his neck as he strode to the bed. 'Do you want it short and abridged?' she teased.

'Uh-uh,' he said, lowering her on to the mattress. 'I want it for the rest of my life. I want you to marry me again.'

Her body froze. To the extent where she couldn't even get her vocal cords to move.

'It'll work this time, Nessa. You know it will,' he urged. 'I realise you won't want to live at Brayburn, because of your career and all. But, well, I figure I could put in a manager to take over the day-to-day running of the place and we could maybe go over a few times each year to check out how things were going. After all, with Angie and the baby living there you'd want to visit every so often anyway.'

Even though her brain had ceased to function normally Vanessa was acutely aware of every word he said. She could hear the love in his voice and the funny mixture of hope and hesitation making his pronunciation less precise than usual. She even identified a tiny nagging doubt edging his tone and it was this sliver of uncertainty that caused her smile to slip.

'Nessa? Honey, what is it?'

'I...I need to know if you've forgiven me for what happened to...to Samuel. If—'

Mitch bolted upright. His face contorted in disbelief and Vanessa felt her entire future happiness fall victim to the past.

'*Forgiven you*? Forgiven *you*?'

He grasped her shoulders to prevent her looking away. Pain tore at her insides as her mind assimilated that she'd asked for the impossible.

'Vanessa, I've *never* blamed you. Never!'

He was watching her face so intently as if trying to read her mind.

'My God! Are you saying you thought I blamed you for what happened?'

She nodded, huge sobs and a torrent of tears preventing words. Mitch swore and pulled her into an embrace so strong she could scarcely breathe.

'Oh, Nessa. Nessa darling.' The uneven timbre of his voice was evidence of the wave of emotion swamping him too. 'I blamed myself. I blamed Rachel. I even blamed God. But I *never ever* blamed you.'

Speech was beyond her; all she could do, to convey what his words meant to her, was to hold him. Hold him every bit as tightly and lovingly as he held her.

'Oh, dear lord, I *never* blamed you...'

His voice broke and an emotive shudder racked his body. It was some minutes before either of them calmed down sufficiently to speak.

When Vanessa finally lifted her head from Mitch's chest, he brushed her hair back from her face, both his touch and eyes tender.

'You OK?' he enquired softly.

She nodded.

'Honey, please believe me. I don't and never have blamed you for what happened.'

'But the first day I was back...when you came after me on the bike, you—'

'I was an emotional wreck. You'd finally come back into my life, but you were telling me that what we'd shared was over. I didn't want to hear that. I wanted to lash out at you.' He took her hands in his and interlocked their fingers. 'I'd always believed you'd left me because you blamed me for Samuel's death. I was desperate to try and make you lift some of the blame from me.'

She sighed and squeezed his hands. 'At first I did blame you, or at least I tried to convince myself it was all your fault,' she admitted. 'But while I was laid up in hospital I had a lot of time to think. Gradually I turned it all back on to me. If I'd been a more complete person, more sophisticated and less dependent on you, you wouldn't have even given Rachel a second glance. If I'd been a more capable rider I wouldn't have been thrown; if I'd been a better mother I'd never have got on the horse in the first place...'

'Oh, hon...'

'It got worse when I came home from hospital. You wouldn't talk to me, you never touched me, you...you scarcely even looked at me.' The remembered loneliness made her shiver. 'I...I thought you hated me.'

Mitch sighed heavily, releasing her hands to rub his face.

'I *couldn't* look at you. The pain and heartbreak in your eyes tore me apart. I kept seeing you lying crumpled on the ground, kept hearing your screams of pain before the paramedics sedated you...' He raised an anguished face to her.

'I kept waiting for you to turn on me—*hoped* that you would. Anything would have been better than watching you withdraw further and further from me in silent suffering. I nearly died the day I came home and found you gone. I went hightailing it after you down to Sydney—'

Her head jerked up. 'You...you came after me?'

He nodded. 'I loved you. I couldn't bear the idea of you not being with me. Even having you there hating me was better than not having you at all.'

Tears again blurred her vision.

'When no one was at your mother's I contacted Cam. After that I didn't know what to do. I didn't know any of your old friends and in the years we were together we only mixed with locals.'

The truth of his words was sadly ironic. He'd hadn't known where to look for her and she hadn't known where to go.

'When your solicitor contacted me three months later, I figured you were better off without me. Buying into Brayburn seemed the only way of making sure you were financially secure.' He shook his head sadly. 'What I should have done was jumped on a plane to Perth the minute I had your address. Everything might have been so different. We wouldn't have lost all these years, wasted so much time.'

'No, Mitch,' she said firmly. 'That's not true. Oh, sure we might have stuck things out together for a little longer, but not permanently.'

For a moment he looked as if he was going to disagree, then he sighed heavily and produced a rueful smile.

'Your "passion not love" theory again, huh?'

'I might have been in my twenties, Mitch, but emotionally I was still a kid.' She spoke with an earnest need to make him understand. 'I'd never grown as a person, not as I should have. I went from being Daddy's little girl to being Mitch's wife and then on to being Angie's mother. I'd never had a chance to find out who Vanessa Brayburn was, much less who Vanessa Randall *could* be.'

'They're one and the same, Nessa,' he said his hand brushing her cheek. 'The woman I love. The woman I've always loved.'

'Yes, but the difference is that now *I* love myself. And that, Mitch Randall—' she kissed his palm '—means I can accept your love so much more easily.'

He groaned, flopping back on to the bed and taking her with him.

'Thank God.' He smiled, drawing her head to his. 'Because you'll be having it foisted on to you for the rest of your life.'

He claimed her mouth with infinite tenderness, his lips and tongue so gentle against hers that Vanessa almost wept. Every kiss held a promise for the future and every touch healed a scar from the past.

In that instant she understood that not only could the human heart *hear* what was unsaid, but that it could also *speak*. And because her heart was completely attuned to Mitch's it recognised every silent apology and unspoken declaration of love he offered.

She was about to verbalise the utter joy she was feeling, but changed her mind. She wanted Mitch to discover what was in her heart on his own.

'Mitch?'

'Mmm,' came the muttered response as his tongue lathed her jaw.

'Can we make love in silence?'

He groaned as she trailed her fingers over his shoulder blades. 'I seriously doubt it.'

'No I don't actually mean *can* we, I mean I want to make love without words.'

The blissful giving action of his mouth stopped immediately, his weight shifting slightly as he raised his head to stare searchingly at her.

'Nessa, it's not as if we usually have a running dialogue at a time like this. So what do you mean? No moans, no groans, no ooohhs and aaahhhs?'

'I mean no talking. Let's not express ourselves verbally.'

'Sort of an "actions speak louder than words" exercise, huh?'

She rolled her head from side to side on the pillow, smiling, 'No, an exercise in listening with our hearts.' She lifted her hand and laid it against Mitch's chest and beneath her fingers felt a drumming rhythm that echoed the intensity of her own heart identically. Her gaze never left Mitch's face as she first raised his right hand to her lips and kissed the tip of each finger, then laid it across her heart.

For several moments he didn't move. Then slowly he lifted a solitary finger to his lips to indicate his participation.

When two tears began to quietly roll down her face, Mitch caught them on his finger and crossed his heart with them.

Their lovemaking on that occasion was unlike any they'd previously shared; languidly soft and ethereal. And its afterglow should have been a time of shared reflection, but Mitch apparently didn't think so. Vanessa had been trying to start a conversation with him for ten minutes to no avail. He'd kiss her, caress her, even tickle her, but he'd not uttered a word.

'You've been lying there with that smirk on your face for nearly twenty minutes. You must have something to say.'

'I'm waiting for your answer,' he said. 'Are you going to marry me?'

She recalled how he'd gone down on one knee all those years ago. Certainly he'd phrased his question more romantically the first time, but she knew that this time she wasn't being asked because Mitch wanted to do the right thing.

'Mitch, you said that you wouldn't have asked me to marry you the first time if I hadn't been pregnant.' She paused for his nod. 'Yet if you wanted me as much as you said you did, then why not?'

'Misguided nobility, I guess. You were only sixteen years old, still at boarding school. Even if I'd "gone with guts" and asked you, there was no way your old man would give legal approval for his daughter to marry an under-educated, flat-broke jackaroo,' he admitted. 'Plus, I couldn't really credit that someone like you could really love me anyway.'

Vanessa sighed, sad that she'd not recognised how insecure Mitch had really been at nineteen; a foolish thought, since she hadn't been able to begin facing her own inadequacies until nearly ten years later.

'Besides,' he added turning his gorgeous blue eyes to her and grinning. 'I was into my "why buy a cow when you can get the milk free" stage!'

'Oh, thanks tons! You rat!' She aimed a furious glare at him, but he laughed and dragged her against his naked hardness.

'However, these days I have absolutely no reservations about asking a highly successful, financially independent woman to be my wife. And,' he stressed, 'I intend to keep asking her until I get the answer I want to hear! So?'

'You already know the answer,' she said, kissing his chin.

'I know,' he said gently. 'Your heart told me. But I wanted to hear it aloud as well. This time round, I'm making damned sure we keep all the lines of communication open.'

'Me too.' She looked lovingly into his eyes. 'There's nothing I want more than to be your wife for the rest of my life. I love you, Mitch Randall...in all ways, for always.'

The proposal was sealed with a kiss that scorched Vanessa's soul. It would work. She didn't have even an atom of doubt that their love was stronger than eternity. Ooohhhh! She felt so complete! So unbelievably happy, she thought she'd die of it. She would! She would most definitely die loving this man!

'You think Angie'd mind if we called her and gave her the good news that her baby isn't going to be an illegitimate grandchild?' Mitch asked a good time later.

'Darling, it's way too late to call the east. Besides, in case you've forgotten, in this country you have to wait four weeks to get married.'

'Not if you apply for permission to have the time shortened.'

She raised an eyebrow at his knowing tone.

He grinned. 'I checked it out today.'

'But there's so much we have to sort out,' she reasoned sensibly. 'Brayburn, the—'

'Forget Brayburn,' he said quickly. 'I understand your first commitment is to the boutique.'

She shook her head. 'No,' she smiled. 'My first commitment is to us. I can have Lou manage the store. She's more than capable.'

'But what about the du Pont deal? You said it yourself, that's a major coup.'

'It would have been if I'd got it.'

'You mean you didn't?'

'Nope.'

'Oh, Nessa, I'm so sorry. I know how much that meant to you. You must feel devastated.'

'Oh, no,' she said passionately. 'I feel like the most loved woman in history.'

'You are, Nessa,' he said, his hand cupping her face. 'Believe me, you are...'

EPILOGUE

VANESSA woke to the incessant burr of the bedroom telephone. Instinctively she tried to reach for it. It took a second to recognise that at Brayburn the phone was on Mitch's side of the bed. Not, she smiled, that he was ever inclined to stay there.

'Mitch?' She stroked his neck.

'Mmm.' His sleepy response belied the firmness of the arm he tightened around her.

'You want to get the phone?'

'Not particularly,' he groaned, opening his eyes to smile at her. 'But I will just for peace.'

He levered himself in sitting position and snatched at the receiver.

'Hello…Craig!'

Vanessa was instantly on her knees in excited expectation.

'Is it Angie? Are they ready to leave for the hospital?'

She watched as Mitch's grin grew wider in his handsome face.

Summing up the situation that Angela had gone in to labour, she was about to spring from the bed when Mitch grabbed her ankle.

'Hey, Nessa,' he grinned. 'We've got a twenty-minute-old granddaughter!'

'What?' Her mind went numb. 'She's had it? *Here*, at…at home? Is she OK? Is the baby OK? Let me talk to her.'

'Calm down, honey, they're both fine.' Mitch manoeuvred to tug her into his arm while still talking on the phone.

'OK, then. Well, congratulations, mate,' he was saying. 'I know exactly how you're feeling and you tell that daughter of mine we're proud of all of you.'

Vanessa was ready to explode with frustration, and when Mitch started laughing at something Craig said she made a lunge for the phone. Frowning with mock anger, he held her at bay.

'Righto, mate. Listen, I'll have to go. I think your mother-in-law is trying to seduce me....'

'*Mitch!*' Vanessa glared at him.

'Yeah, good idea! These Randall women have a history of impulsive passion. OK, mate, catch up with you shortly.'

He hung up the phone grinning like a Cheshire cat. Then pulled her into his arms and bestowed an enormous kiss on her. It distracted her only momentarily.

'Tell me,' she demanded when they came up for air.

'Angie went into labour last night while she and Craig were in town having dinner.'

'They should have phoned and told us,' she said without any genuine annoyance.

'Well, believe it or not, the doctors managed to bluff their way through it without you,' he teased.

She hit him in the ribs. 'A girl, huh? Did Craig say what they were going to call her?'

'Nope. The poor guy's was more interested in finding out if I knew the number of the nearest closed order of nuns.' He touched the lines of her frown with a finger. 'Given the impulsive passion in her female blood-lines, he's not taking any chances and wants to book his firstborn into a convent a.s.a.p.'

'Idiot!' she accused, but Mitch was staring bemusedly at the ceiling.

'You know, I can't believe how lucky I am,' he marvelled. 'I'm only thirty-eight years old and yet I've got everything a man could want in a lifetime already.' He turned to look at her. 'A wife who loves me more than any man could ever dream of, a daughter who had the good sense to fall in love with a bloke I approve oof—'

'Only,' Vanessa put in, 'because he's practically a reincarnation of you!'

'Ssh,' he said. 'Don't interrupt. And a brand new granddaughter I'll live long enough to watch grow up. I didn't dream I could feel this happy.'

'I did,' she said as she blinked back tears. 'I just didn't think it could happen until recently.'

'Ah, Nessa.' He lowered his lips to hers and instantly Vanessa's tongue responded to the thrill of his, but she allowed herself to enjoy the divine sensations he created for only a few moments before forcing herself to break free and scoot from the bed.

'C'mon, I want to get dressed and go see our new granddaughter. Before Eleanor Super-Granny O'Brien beats me to it.'

Mitch stayed on the bed, chuckling with mirth.

Opening a drawer, Vanessa rummaged through an assortment of underwear before selecting a navy blue lace camisole with matching French knickers. She pulled them on and looked up to find Mitch watching her with a look of pure seduction. Liquid heat consumed her.

'I don't think grandpas are supposed to have such lustful thoughts, Mitch Randall,' she said, feeling her nipples spring to attention under his gaze.

'It's your fault, *Nanna* Randall,' he said, tossing the sheet aside.

The sheer beauty of his naked masculinity as he moved towards her weakened her knees.

'If you expect me to think of you in grandmotherly terms you shouldn't wear such damn sexy underwear. I hate to say it,' he said, sliding the straps from her shoulders with deliciously slow fingers, 'but these have definitely got to go.'

Vanessa laughed.

'You have a problem with that, Nanna Randall?'

'Uh-uh, Grandpa Randall,' she said slipping her arms around his neck. 'Not one.'

And, as they kissed, Vanessa sensed the excitement and happiness each of them felt flow into the other and multiply. And she knew Mitch's heart was hearing the messages of her own, and always would... That was what happened when passion progressed to love...

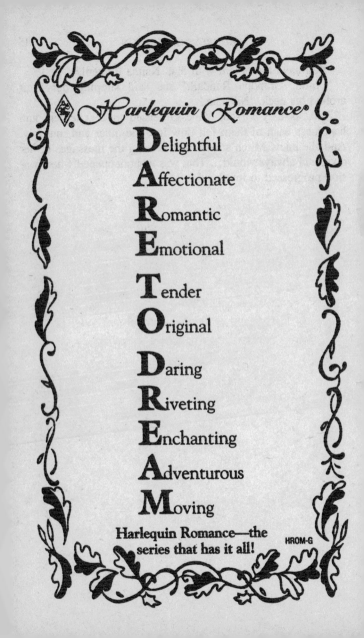

Harlequin Romance®

Delightful

Affectionate

Romantic

Emotional

Tender

Original

Daring

Riveting

Enchanting

Adventurous

Moving

Harlequin Romance—the
series that has it all!

HROM-G

Harlequin® Historical

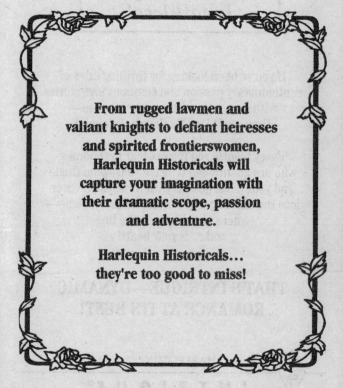

From rugged lawmen and
valiant knights to defiant heiresses
and spirited frontierswomen,
Harlequin Historicals will
capture your imagination with
their dramatic scope, passion
and adventure.

Harlequin Historicals...
they're too good to miss!

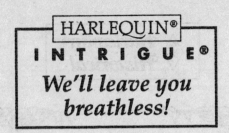

HARLEQUIN®

I N T R I G U E®

We'll leave you breathless!

If you've been looking for thrilling tales of
contemporary passion and sensuous love stories
with taut, edge-of-the-seat suspense—
then you'll *love* **Harlequin Intrigue!**

Every month, you'll meet four new heroes
who are guaranteed to make your spine tingle
and your pulse pound. With them you'll enter
into the exciting world of Harlequin Intrigue—
where your life is on the line
and so is your heart!

THAT'S INTRIGUE—DYNAMIC ROMANCE AT ITS BEST!

HARLEQUIN®

I N T R I G U E®

INT-GENR

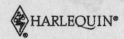

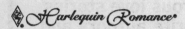

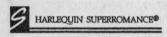

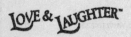